HERO

FREDERICK G. DILLEN

STEERFORTH PRESS

SOUTH ROYALTON, VERMONT

Library of Congress Cataloging-in-Publication Data
Dillen, Frederick G., 1946–
Hero : a novel / by Frederick G. Dillen.
p. cm.
ISBN 1–883642–19–1
I. Title.
PS3554.I45H47 1994
813'.54—dc20 94–13981

Manufactured in the United States of America

Third Printing

To my wife Leslie, and my daughters Abigail and Tatiana

G.A.D. — God bless him and keep him, and tell him please
that I asked to say hello

HERO

The first day in his new steakhouse he trailed another waiter to learn the service, and as he followed that waiter up the stairs from the basement kitchen, the waiter stumbled and upset a shouldered tray. Pops, or Dad, or whoever he would become, put a hand up and balanced the tray for the waiter. A third waiter saw it happen, and called out, "The new guy is a hero. Hero, listen, I want you to follow me from now on and catch my trays."

The steakhouse was in mid-town Manhattan and was expensive, and on Sundays there was no business. Hero was the new man so he got the lousy shifts, and on one Sunday night the barman brought in a television with a screen the size of someone's hand. It was October and the World Series, and Hero looked at it from across and behind the barman. If any of the other waiters had wanted to look at it, Hero would have gone without a thought back to his station or to sit in the kitchen, but the other waiters were foreign or were gay and didn't look at baseball.

On the screen the third baseman punched his glove, and had a chew of tobacco the size of a golf ball in the right side of his mouth, and squirted spit again and again at the dirt. The barman kept the sound low enough that Hero did not have to hear the commentators talk, but the camera and the little screen looked at the third baseman, and Hero looked at the third

1

baseman. And because even the World Series held no more interest than any other program for Hero, in another moment Hero would have drifted away.

There was a high foul ball, however, and the third baseman ran full speed at the dugout which fell in four, sharp, concrete steps to the line of the third baseman's own teammates. At the last moment, the third baseman dropped to the seat of his pants and slid full force over the edge of the concrete steps, and, with the chew squeezed in the side of his face, watched the foul ball down into his glove, and then was hurtling among his teammates who tried to catch him and tried to keep his head from breaking open as it whipped back onto the concrete. The third baseman's arms flailed from his washboard rush down the steps, and as he finished in a heap among the feet and the crouched uniforms of his teammates, the ball popped carelessly free. Up out of the heap, the third baseman stood slowly. His hat was off. His chew was in place. His teammates and coaches touched at him and asked at him and he nodded absently and reached down and picked up his hat and put that on and looked out to the field, shook his head slightly, climbed slowly up two of the dugout steps, and was plainly not a boy with rubber limbs but a grown man who hurt. He stepped up the last two steps of the dugout and jogged out to his position at third base and punched his glove and spat and bent to give his concentration at the batter who readied for the next pitch.

"Hero." There was a party of two at the desk. The maître d' and the floor manager were downstairs in the office looking at a real television, and the old Iranian, the waiter who had taken the desk, summoned Hero. Hero now would have stayed to see more of the game, but it would never have occurred to him to say so, and he stood away from the bar.

"No," the Bolivian said. "Hero doesn't want a deuce. Hero's American. He's watching the World Series. Hero's rooting for the Americans in the championship of the world only Americans play. Give the deuce to a foreigner, or one of the girls."

"You think South Americans don't play baseball?" the Iranian said. "You think the Carribeans don't play baseball? What's the matter with you? Bolivian."

"Don't talk to me about South America, Camel Driver."

"No wonder you can't run your country. You can't even read your own sports pages. You don't know what happens in your own village."

"Don't talk to me about my country, Ayatollah."

The Polack came at them, saying, "Listen to the Ayatollah. He knows baseball. He is going to start his own Iranian team and beat the American pigs."

"Shut up, Polack. I'm talking to the Bolivian mother now. When I am done with him then I will tell you about what a piece of dung is your homeland. Solidarity, I spit on it."

The Bolivian called loudly, "Ayatollah and the Polack. Khomeini and Martina."

"You think I am going to listen to you?" the Polack said to the Iranian. "Old man? You come from the desert, you wipe with your fingers, you cook with camel shit. I am civilized."

"What? Nobody reads in your village either? No schools? No history? I'll tell you. Everybody pisses in Poland's pot, from Ghengis Khan to Breshnev. Ignorant Polack. What do you know about civilization? I'll tell . . ."

The deuce was in and one of the gays had taken it, and on television now the third baseman was sitting on the bench in the dugout, laughing with the guy beside him. The third baseman took off his hat and felt the back of his head and then bent his head and offered it to the next guy who touched it and laughed. A couple of the other guys reached over to feel the back of his head, and then the third baseman looked up at them and laughed again, and they laughed with him. He had a good face. When he laughed, he laughed.

"You're a fan, Hero. I didn't know you were a fan. I watch the Series here in Manhattan and I feel like I'm watching it in Sri Lanka or something, you know what I mean?" The bartender said that, and Hero stood back a step from the bar. He put a hand in his pocket to touch his keys.

When he was up, the third baseman only topped a grounder that rolled under the pitcher's glove. Still there was no play, and he was on with a single.

"Good hustle," the barman said.

Hero was no fan, and no athlete. That he watched at all was as odd and passing as anger. But his next time up the third baseman hit a double and drove in two runs, and Hero slapped his hand on the bar as the third baseman hit the dirt off his pants and worked his chew and spat and took his lead.

His last time up, he lined a single and drove in the winning run. It was not the last game of the Series, but it was a Series game just the same, and he'd won it, and when he ran off the field with his teammates he lost all his concentration and was a boy with all the rest of his team, all of them delighted in a bunch. In front of the camera, inside the clubhouse, he laughed out and shouted in a whoop over at someone outside the picture, and then turned and pointed down the clubhouse over the heads of his teammates and laughed and whooped again.

"Hey, Polack," the Bolivian called. "Hey, Khomeini. Look at the Hero. The Americans must have lost."

The announcer was calling him back, pointing after the third baseman and waving him back.

"Hero is crying."

He was not sobbing. Not tears running down his face.

"The Camel Drivers beat the Americans in the World Series."

He thought to go into the kitchen. He wiped his face and made his invisible smile. He knew it was best just to go away, yet he waited to see if the third baseman would come back for the announcer.

"Leave him alone," the Iranian said. "Ignorant Bolivian."

"It was Polack National Team that wins," the Polack shouted. "Iranians throw like girls. Everybody sees that from the embassy."

4

"You think we didn't beat the Americans, Polack? Ask Carter. Who did Solidarity ever beat?"

The third baseman stepped back up onto the platform with the announcer and, grinning, chew still deforming his plain handsome face, pulled off his hat and bent his head forward and flattened his hair to show the lump from his fall.

Instead of whatever else he should have said or done, Hero pointed at the tiny screen and said, "You want to see an American?"

And the Bolivian and the Polack and the Iranian, instead of laughing, or instead of ignoring Hero, stepped over to look. They cared about an American, even if Hero did not. Hero felt for his keys again, and despite himself he remembered the last summer he was a father — throwing fly balls in backyard evenings to a World Series announced by his youngest boy, announced in a voice still years from changing. On green, darkening grass he played catch wearing his older son's, his wrong son's, discarded mitt, with Alice calling them in because she knew he couldn't see in the dark. She knew the balls that came back at him from their good boy were more than awkward; she knew they frightened him. She knew every weakness, and called him in, and he went in, furious and thirsty, leaving grass to the night.

The third baseman was nodding, neither patronizing the announcer nor taking himself as seriously as the announcer wanted. The third baseman smiled with a frank, open, blessedly regular smile. He smiled for an instant at the camera and at the men — no different than him, his smile seemed to say — at Hero, the barman, the Iranian, the Bolivian, and the Polack, all of whom looked back at that third baseman in silence.

LITANY

The true Hero was as unseen by everyone else as by himself. He was part of this steakhouse which worked with two-man teams of waiters, with no busboys, and with rolling push-carts which each night were covered with tablecloths and marked with their waiters' names. Guéridons they were called, and served the purposes of trays and auxiliary busing stands.

In the front of the restaurant was a long bar with stools, and then in the body of the restaurant were tables for a hundred and twenty. The kitchen was two stories. On the same floor as the dining room were bread drawers, an ice box for chilling salad plates, the *bain marie* for soups, and the station for the salad man who also did cold desserts. These things were just behind the doors to the dining room. At a turn, leading away from the dining room, was the walkway through to the stairs down to the hot kitchen, and parallel with this walkway was the long dish-washers' counter with its flat stainless basin for dishes and its overhead shelf for glass-racks and the bin underneath for silver next to the tubs for garbage. Beyond was an open alcove lined with extra sinks, espresso pots, and stainless heating cabinets for plates. Between shifts the guéridons were parked in this alcove. Before a shift, waiters sat here among the guéridons which by then were linened and marked with their back men's names for the coming service. Across, along the long wall of the walkway, was a thicket of ice buckets as well as extra, upended glass-racks and the couple of rubber pails of ice brought up for the service. Then came the open door to those stairs which pitched down at the hot kitchen below.

Hero led this general layout through his mind in sequence with the rest. There was an equation in every restaurant which told where the customer went and when and what the customer got, and which told also how the food was ordered and how serviced and delivered and retrieved. There were ways to lubricate this equation, but Hero was not someone who could charm or manipulate his customers. Hero did not ask for help from other waiters or assert himself when he needed lobster cocktails fast. He could not play to the touchy self-esteem of the broiler man when a meat was to be done peculiarly. Because of these things, Hero had to know his restaurant's equation perfectly, and it was that perfect equation which made Hero's litany.

As a dishwasher, it had only been simpler. As a dishwasher, there had been big plates, little plates, cups, saucers, glasses, silverware, rinse, slop, racks, track, machine and run and pull free. A steady choreography that ran through his head without end, on shift and off, through successions of furnished rooms, through years and successions of restaurants.

As a waiter, the litany, umbilical with its course of physical responses, became only more elaborate for Hero. The price of every item, the preparation of every item, the pattern of service, the ritual of ordering at the bar and of ordering from the hot kitchen and ordering from the cold man, of stocking the cart, of handing to the back man, of timing the tables, of knowing the wine stock, of knowing the steps from table to table, of knowing which condiment, which fork, which sauce. Hero knew it all, every possible step of service for every possible customer, every functional inch of the restaurant. This was his only memory, and now with so many compartments and components to it, saying the whole litany to himself became an occupation of parts. Appetizers. Desserts. Morning and afternoon. Laundromat and subway and back.

If Hero's variations as a waiter were to become more simple again even than those of a dishwasher, if there were only one thing for him to do, one word, Hero would play that one word through himself in constant repetition.

In this particular steakhouse, however, there was an added aspect to the rigor of Hero's litany. In this steakhouse the hot kitchen was downstairs, and with the two-man teams of waiters, one waiter was the front man and one was the back man. It was the back man's job to bring up the food. The front man worked the dining room and the upstairs kitchen, but rarely went downstairs and did not ever have to carry the trays of food upstairs. Hero was a front man. Hero was too old to carry trays of loaded plates up twenty-two red, cement steps, and yet despite the appearances of its address and its bright dining room, this was a restaurant where there was no hesitation to damage. It was a restaurant where the waiters' basement locker room was wet and unlit, under a sidewalk beyond the baling machine for garbage. It was a restaurant where the bathroom, the one toilet for all of them except the managers and customers, did not flush; waiters coming from the locker room went single file against the cornering wall around the sour puddle that spread from the bathroom's swollen door.

This was a restaurant where the owner was unknown and Fat Tom the general manager was glimpsed only before those services when someone was squeezed out. If Fat Tom learned that Hero could not properly work the front, then the next shift Hero would work the back. If Hero could not work the back, one way or another, he would be gone. And just as the general manager here, and the floor manager and the maître d', saw Hero as old, so everyone else saw him old also, too old perhaps now. The next restaurants would not get nicer. Perhaps it would be that he'd wash dishes again. Maybe the truth was that Hero did not want to have to wash dishes again, though he would not ever have thought to say so. He touched the keys to his building, his rooms and his mailbox, and then the litany of appetizers drowned out all possibilities but its own. Lobster cocktail, eleven dollars, cold plate, cold cover plate, cocktail fork, shelling crackers, cocktail sauce, green sauce, hot damp napkin.

In the hour before the dinner service, the hour for staff meals, two immigrant Chinese dishwashers had their dinners behind the stainless steel counter which was still littered with the last plates and foods and liquids from the end of lunch service. The older Chinese ate quietly enough, but the young Chinese ate almost without utensils and made noises with his mouth which were so loud and so gurgling and forcing as either to come from another species or from some awful violence with a knife.

Hero sat and stared at his own hands on his own knees, and at the slick red floor beneath his black shoes. The hands were an old man's hands, veined and livered and yellow-nailed, yet still strong. Still some way pink and clean and delicate, regardless of the stubby appearance of strength. Though what had he ever used them for? They were his hands, recognizably.

A new waiter, a tall, pale boy with glasses, came up from the hot kitchen with his dinner and smiled around at the other waiters who ate and lounged among the guéridons. None of the other waiters looked at the boy — Andy was his name. Hero, too, had his eyes down again between his knees by the time Andy had gotten to him as a possibility for a dinner partner. Though it had never occurred to anyone to sit by Hero to eat their dinner. Or if ever it had occurred to anyone, it had never registered with Hero who, tonight as most nights, sat by himself along the wall among the ice buckets, on one of the extra, upended glass-racks.

Andy pulled a chair to join the young Chinese dishwasher. The older Chinese ate standing up over the open garbage from lunch, but the younger Chinese had the end of an empty cart, a linened but unclaimed guéridon, pulled into the end of their stainless alcove, and Andy sat gingerly to the other end of that guéridon.

"Do you mind if I sit here with you?"

The Chinese did not lift his head, but Hero noticed the other waiters watching. Beginning to grin, some of them.

"How are you tonight?" Andy said, in a happy, trying, blond, young voice, pushing up his glasses and actually looking at the Chinese as if he expected a conversation. The Chinese moved his face lower to his food.

"It's not bad," Andy said, and even the waiters with newspapers had put those down.

The Bolivian, just as he opened his mouth to speak, glanced over and caught Hero watching, caught Hero's eye in fact. The Bolivian was pleased to have found Hero watching, and worked his grin at Hero, and then looked again over at Andy and the Chinese. "Chino," the Bolivian said. "Chino. Why don't you talk to Andy? Don't you like Andy, Chino? Don't you think Andy's cute?"

The Chinese turned his head and, almost without a break in his eating, with his head still as low as it had been, said a sound which came out like a guttural, "Fuck," and which came out also with the rice and the grease and a shred of chicken tendon.

In a group, the waiters laughed, and Andy, who at first stared amazed at the spit on the guéridon's top-cloth, now looked over at the other waiters' laughter. Andy smiled himself. It was an unsure smile, but just the same Andy turned back at the Chinese and managed an assertion of the smile which suggested shyly that Andy was part of the waiters and was laughing with them at the Chinese. The Chinese took no notice, and in another moment had finished utterly his food. The instant he finished he stood, stepped to his long, broad counter-sink, and tossed his plate in with the other plates left from lunch and now from the staff dinner. He pulled the rinse gun from its holder and began spraying, separating out silver, sliding with his free hand the loose slop of food to the round drainage in the counter or to the tub of garbage beneath.

Andy watched this, and then looked back to the waiters with his smile, a stronger smile now, a smile of friends and common ground. The waiters sat in the clustered traffic of their guéridons, and the newspapers and the magazines were back up, and there was no one to meet Andy's smile even among those whose only occupation in this hour before the service was watching for action. Andy turned with his smile then around to Hero, and Hero too disappeared for Andy. So that when Hero looked up again, Andy was eating alone on that guéridon which was littered with the spray from the Chinese's feeding. The Bolivian was looking then too, however, and again the Bolivian caught Hero's eye. And again grinned. As if the Bolivian and Hero were in together on a dirty, amusing mischief.

Hero was not. Hero went out from the kitchen, to stand alone in the dining room at his station.

WORK

"Go crazy, Hero," O'Meara said under his breath as he helped Hero pull out the table for a party of three. "Enjoy your dinners," O'Meara said then to the three, and unbuttoned the sport jacket that was tight across his stomach, and strolled back at the desk.

"Would you like me to check your coat for you?" Hero said to the woman who sat in the banquette at the end of the table.

She had a full length sable over her shoulders, and she said, "I'm quite comfortable."

But when Hero came back with drinks the same woman said, as though it were something she'd asked before, "Couldn't you turn down the heat?"

The Iranian, who was front man at the next station, snorted. Hero bent at the woman as he delivered her drink, and said, "I'll try to get it turned down."

Hero walked with a solid, balanced gait, but always climbed the three steps to the bar cautiously. On his next time up those steps, and past the desk, he paused and said to O'Meara, the floor manager, "The woman on twenty-six would like to have the heat turned down."

O'Meara looked over. Chick, the maître d', standing with his tuxedo jacket flared, looked also. O'Meara smiled. "In the sable, Hero?"

Hero nodded. He had moved to the service end of the bar a few paces away from them.

O'Meara laughed and Chick said, "If she can't afford to check it, Hero, tell her to sell it."

"I think she wants to keep it on," Hero said quietly, but O'Meara and Chick were looking across at the woman and laughing again. "Where do you find them?" O'Meara said as if to Hero. Then he said to Chick as though Hero were not in hearing, "Fucking Hero," and Chick and O'Meara grinned out the finish of their laughter.

When he opened the menu for her the woman in the coat looked at Hero and said loudly, "What is the matter here? I'm far too hot."

Behind the post that backed the woman's banquette, the Iranian, taking shrimp off his guéridon, made a noise of phlegm for the woman. She glared at Hero, who folded gently from his middle and silently offered her the round blotching pinkness that was the top of his head.

"I don't want to check my coat," the woman said fiercely to Hero. "God knows what would happen to it in your checkroom. I want you to turn down the heat."

Hero kept his head inclined to the woman and nodded and then departed as if in her behalf. The next time he went to the bar he told O'Meara again.

Chick saw Hero speak to O'Meara, and came grinning. "She still hot, Hero?"

Hero stood over in line at the bar, holding his corked bar tray and checking his glasses for the proper fruit. O'Meara said, "Pour water on her, Hero. I don't want to hear about it again."

As Hero turned away with drinks for his other tables, the Iranian came after him to the bar. "Feed her to the revolution," the Iranian said. "Give her to the mob, she thinks she's so hot," and Hero climbed with his studied pretense of ease down the three steps from the bar to the restaurant floor.

He went to stand next to the woman, facing along the table with her, and bent again at his waist. There was something royally polite about even the bone stiffness of his posture, as if here were a conspiracy of domestic intrigue between a circumspect, arthritic butler and a mistress of considerable elegance. It was the instinct and the willingness for this kind of posture that kept Hero a front man. "Perhaps I could hang your sable over the back of one of these chairs, Madam. And cover it with a tablecloth to protect it."

"Oh for God's sake," the woman said. Hero did not move from his bow, and did not glance to any of them at the table. "Well, take it," she said. "Take it." And Hero helped her out of the coat and smoothed the coat and folded the coat gently and tenderly over the back of one of the chairs outside the table. Then he went to the busing stand for a large tablecloth and folded that carefully and completely about the coat.

"Ahh," came the voice of the Iranian from somewhere in the next station.

Another waiter, a back man, swerved close to the table with a guéridon loaded with dirty dishes, and the woman said sharply to Hero, "You're going to have to do better than this."

"Perhaps I could lay the coat across the seats of both of these chairs. Then it would be protected by the backs of the chairs."

"Why don't you just turn the heat down. How about that?"

"Ahh," the Iranian called again from his distance, and the woman turned away from Hero who stretched the coat carefully over the seats of the two chairs and covered the coat again and brought another tablecloth to make the covering more secure.

When she was almost to the end of her main course, the woman called, "Waiter."

Hero came and once more stood beside her and bowed low to hear her. The Iranian, passing with a bottle of wine, hesitated to hear also.

"You know," she said, "that if you spill this grease as you clear our plates, all your tablecloths are not going to keep my coat from being ruined. That much should be apparent. Yes? Do you understand why we have to take care of the coat? Speak to me."

Hero would ordinarily have remained in his bow long enough for the woman to recognize more than humility, long enough for her to understand his physical discomfort too, his anxiety about the coat to the point of pain. And then he would have nodded, all in silence, and then taken each plate with the most gracious care.

But the new waiter, Andy, came with a guéridon. And because Andy could not yet cleanly stack a guéridon or steer a right course, because the Iranian still stood nearby witnessing the progress of the coat, Hero had to straighten to let Andy pass.

Instead of passing, he looked at Hero with concern. He said, "Are you okay? I saw you bent over." Hero nodded to him, and Andy stood and Hero nodded again, pointedly. "Oh," Andy said, and pushed his guéridon on for the kitchen, and Hero bowed once more, and remained in his bow as though he might be too stiff to get up.

What Hero didn't do was remain silent. Rather, he spoke quietly toward the floor, just loud enough for the woman to hear. He said, "Tickle your ass with a feather."

For a moment she was quiet, and the other two at the table also were quiet.

After that one moment, the woman said in a voice mixed of amazement, fury, and confusion, "What?"

The other two at the table were startled by the tone of her voice, and so was Hero. He stood up half out of his bow and looked at her. "Particularly harassing weather," he said. "Outside. That's why we've got to watch this coat so carefully." He looked now admiringly at the mummied sable, and in his face was all the slow, purposeful ignorance of every waiter's doomed attempt to say the right thing.

FRIENDS

Hero had never said anything like that before, and would say nothing like it again. Once it had happened, he might as well never have said it at all, and that finally was what the other waiters believed despite the Iranian's story. The Iranian shouted at Hero's dumb refusal of what had actually been said, and Hero disappeared gratefully behind the noise of the Iranian's shouting.

With his hawked nose and his white mustache, the Iranian liked to flaunt the expressions of a man made fierce by age; his eyes searched the world for offenses to his dignity, and for opportunities to punish those offenses. He took pleasure in this operation of indignity and redress, and when he screamed at the other waiters, the other waiters enjoyed him.

Now, once or twice a night, in passing Hero, the Iranian snorted with unspoken amusement to let Hero know that the incident of the sable would not be forgotten, and that he, the Iranian, remained satisfied with the incident and with Hero. It began even to seem that the Iranian interpreted Hero's silence as a variety of dignity, and so beyond the snorts there came slight, formal nods. And beyond all this, the Iranian seemed ready for something which was more unsettling than a false assignment of dignity. Occasionally, in his nods of respect, the

Iranian allowed what — tenderness? — into his eyes. At those times it was as if the Iranian — Hussein was his name — suspected in Hero something as unfathomable as loneliness, which Hussein might be prepared to answer with friendship.

When he saw, no matter how he tried not to see, whatever was in the Iranian's look, Hero felt the depth of his own silence thinning, and out of that less capable silence a figure emerged. As he recognized the figure, Hero felt an emptiness of defeat and a giddiness someone else might have mistaken for pleasure. He touched through his pocket at his keys. He pulled his silence around himself with a determination that had not been necessary before, and he turned away from the figure, from his own shape.

It was a shape which may not always have been short, but was now a common size among most of the waiters except the Americans. Puffiness from alcohol was not even a memory, but there was a roundness to him from his short, sturdy legs to his jowls. Whether he was on a shift or was lost in the invisible stillness between shifts, some slow anxiety worked in the muscles of his jaw, and so there was a bulging on each side of his face as if he had nuts in the back of his cheeks. The top of his head contributed also to the roundness. His only hair was in a narrow band reaching around the back of his head from ear to ear, and because there were darker, varying shades of grey shot through the white, that hair appeared more coarse than the hair for most heads. Hair at once so little and so apparently coarse made his round, bare crown that much more delicate and vulnerable. As well as sturdy legs, he had thick hands and short arms, and a solid, round-bellied trunk; yet it was the round, humble vulnerability of that exposed crown which gave what lasting impression was to be taken of his presence.

His eyes were bright and quite blue, and they were surrounded by a radiance of deep, now sagging creases, as if from years of squinting, or, more, as if from much laughter. But they were eyes which never gave and never asked. He had a small, fine, bowed mouth, a plump, cleft chin, a firm nose. For some reason, despite so punishingly much alcohol for so many years, the nose was not swollen or blackened, not even demonstrably broken. His was a face which might have been handsome in its young manhood, and it was not an unattractive face now, for someone nearly seventy. Empty of care and seated above a body still able to do physical work, his face looked to be the face of someone younger than his age, a face which might be jolly with busy retirement. As with the eyes, however, this was not a face which expressed. The bare, blank, humble crown expressed all there was, when the world chose to notice.

What purely expressed the restaurant was the moment in every busy night when there was nothing but frenzied intensity of bar and kitchen and customer and wrong order and failed espresso and pocketed charge slips all in a blur. Normalcy obtained in that busiest moment of the night's service.

Earlier, in the wait for the first customers, there was time for lounging and talking.

"But you want to know what drove her crazy?" Jim said. "I'll give you a clue. I did it with my tongue."

Jim was just back after recovering from too many drugs, too much booze, a bad marriage, and no work as an actor. Everyone was happy to have Jim back, and understood that he would be gone again in another night. Jim was also American, so it was the American waiters who answered him.

"I'm not interested in your Carribbean sexcapades," Henke said, leafing through his *Time*. "Put it in a manual for straight sex in the islands." Henke had had real jobs and now was going through business school; he was aloof, gay, and petulant.

"Don't be coy, Henke," Robert said. "Tell her, Jim. Tell the coy bitch what you did." Robert was the street gay, emaciated and confrontational and smart, and the butt of vicious laughter.

The other American, Bruce, was gay as well, a great, gangling, puppyish man with a benign, rubber face. Frankenstein, they called him. Tonight he was down by the doors to the dining room, sitting on the bread warmer and talking with Hussein, the Iranian. Bruce swung his legs against the warmer lackadaisically, but he kept an ear tuned to the action among the other waiters, there among the guéridons each with its back man's name scrawled proprietarily across its linen.

"You can call your manual," Henke said, "How I Won Back My Wife With Hardly A Word."

"I put my tongue in her asshole, Henke. She went crazy."

All the waiters among the guéridons grinned. They were Henke and Robert, and the Bolivian — Fedy Llosa was his name — and the Mexican, and Castro the Cuban. The Polack was over now with Bruce and Hussein and the Haitian salad man they called Aids. The two Chinese-American waiters, Bogart and his back man Eddie Loo, were off. The Yugoslav and the old Frenchman were out on the floor stealing one another's spare silver for resets. And Andy, Andy too was sitting with the waiters among the guéridons, trying to look ready to say something if something were asked of him.

Hero sat on an empty glass-rack along the creamed brick wall opposite the dishwashing counter and the guéridons, between the doors to the dining room, on one hand, and the door to the stairs down at the hot kitchen on the other. Because Fedy Llosa, the Bolivian, was beginning to look erratically around the kitchen, Hero kept his eyes low.

"You wouldn't believe how she liked it. She went like this, like a crab, across the bed. Look, Henke. She couldn't stand it. I jammed her with my tongue, and when she got to the wall and couldn't go any farther, she screamed. She'd never had anything like it before."

"Frankenstein." The Mexican called at Bruce with a voice that was still thick despite all the years in New York. "You hear what you're missing? Jim is talking about what you like."

"Don't bother us, old Mexican," the Iranian shouted back. "We're having a decent motherfucking conversation. Are you a pervert now, too?"

"That's right," Bruce said in a loud and too happy voice. "All your talk over there is disgusting, and I and my friend Hussein are both revolted. Jimmy, I want you to stop telling these tales. You know perfectly well they're not true."

Bruce paused, and then asked, "What did it taste like?"

"Frankenstein."

"Frankenstein says, What did it taste like."

Howls of laughter came from all the waiters, and bursting within the laughter were shouts of sympathetic lewdness. Rising loudest out of the laughter and above the other shouts, was the voice of the Bolivian, Fedy Llosa, who only echoed at first what the others were shouting, but echoed it with an excitement which was at its own fervent level. "Look," Fedy shouted. "Frankenstein is licking his lips."

Ordinarily Fedy was a simple, coarse weight moving through his chores. Everyone understood, however, that a nerve was always ready for manic arousal.

"Oh, Robert," Bruce said mildly, but in a voice loud enough to carry attention. He got up from the bread drawers and wandered back at the larger group of waiters.

"Don't Oh Robert me," Robert said.

"Oh, Robert," Bruce said. "Now look what you've done. You've gotten Fedy wound up."

"Don't start with me," Robert said. "I'm in no mood for it."

"Listen. Listen to me," Fedy said.

"You see," Bruce said. "You egged it all on, and now look at poor Fedy Llosa."

"Listen," the Bolivian shouted, and stood up, but he was frothing too much with the fever of his own humor to say more.

"Bruce, you're starting with me," Robert said. "It was your fault, and Princess Henke's fault."

"It was your fault, Robert," Henke said, with a prim yawn. "Everything is your fault."

"Shut up." The Bolivian's voice, Fedy's voice, came full strength, suddenly so loud and so rabid as to be entirely commanding.

"Here we go," Bruce said, and rolled his eyes. Henke put down his *Time* to watch. The old Frenchman came in from the dining room and stood there by the doors with his forearm at a right angle across his chest and his linen napkin hanging in a clean line down in front of his stomach.

"Now I am too horny," Fedy shouted over all their heads. "I can't stand it any longer."

Robert stood up. "Keep away from me," he said. "You freak."

"I can't wait for later in the bathroom, Robert. I know how you like the smell down there, how you like to kneel in a wet floor and have your head over everybody's toilet. But with all this talking, I have to have it now. I have to fuck you in the ass right here."

Fedy's voice was stretched to a flat, high, nasal slur with a guttural barking at the consonant stops. And if the voice was frantic beyond its joke, the man's body was the same. He was low and thick and ordinarily slack, but now his back curled with intensity. He had a short neck and a large head, much of which was a broad, outsize jaw, and his hair was black and flat and low to his eyes. Jaw, head, hair, pulled spine, all were part of the rigid body.

"Don't you dare touch me," Robert said loudly but without alarm, as the Bolivian came through the guéridons at him. Robert worked a street-wise disdain into his face and showed that around at the other waiters, whose laughter went on at him and at the Bolivian.

From the door, without disrupting the line of his napkin, the old Frenchman cried, "Get him. Get the faggot." Then the Frenchman tried to laugh as if he found it all as funny as the other waiters.

Robert turned away, and Fedy came up against his back, gripped his hips from behind and began to hump. Robert should have appeared frail, with his bony shoulders and railed legs, but even as he purposefully relaxed against Fedy's assault, the shrewdness in Robert's face dispelled any possibility of frailty.

Both of them were in their black shoes, black pants, white shirts and white waiter's shortcoats. Robert was without his bow tie yet and was as sallow as his limp shirt and his dirtied shortcoat, but Fedy even had his tie clipped into his collar. Perfectly dressed to serve, the Bolivian stood up on the toes of his thick shoes, his head rounding out of his shoulders, and from where a neck should have been, there originated brutal, spasmodic waves that coursed down his humped spine like something electric turning into size and weight until it became pelvic thrusts.

"I love it, Robert. It's so great, Robert." The Bolivian looked over his shoulder for the other waiters, and in the frenzy of his show he seemed hardly able to register their laughter.

"I can't feel it," Robert said.

But in fact the Bolivian could register the laughter, and could register other things as well. He had caught Andy's eye, and was grinning now at Andy.

"Is it too small?" Robert said. "Or can't you get it up? I can do better than this in New Rochelle."

"You're too ugly and too skinny and your asshole is too small. You know who I really want? And you know who really wants me, even more than you do, Robert?"

Andy smiled, still trying to show in his face that he was having fun like everyone else. The Bolivian left Robert, and in a moment was behind Andy's chair, pushing Andy up out of it.

"I saw you looking, Andy. I know you like it. I'm going to do it how you like it."

Andy was on his feet and Fedy Llosa was fitting up behind him. Andy, still with his smile, looked around to the other waiters for a sense of what was happening, or maybe even for help. The waiters laughed. At the other end of the kitchen, Hussein, the Iranian, said, "Let the motherfucking kid alone," but then walked out into the dining room with the Polack. The Bolivian was onto Andy now like a short cur screwing for cruelty a timid giraffe.

Andy looked to Hero.

Hero could have nothing for him, but Andy seemed in desperation to see some chance in Hero. Andy stood with the Bolivian hooked against his back, and begged Hero silently. How could anyone imagine that Hero would have help to offer? The Bolivian looked the other way at the waiters to enjoy his success with them, and Andy wanted anything at all from Hero. Not even help, just for Hero to tell him in some way that it would be all right. Andy looked at Hero, and Hero knew it. A nod would have done.

Through his own pants pocket, Hero felt the edges of his keys against his leg. He looked invisibly back down between his own hands and knees to his own black shoes on the damp, red cement.

And Chick came in the door from the dining room, past the old Frenchman.

"Okay," Chick said. "Let's break up the party. We've got customers in the restaurant. I want waiters on the floor. Fedy, leave the new guy alone. He's a kid, for Christ sake."

"I had to fuck him in the ass, Chick."

"I don't want to hear about it. And keep away from me. Out on the floor, all of you assholes."

BEAUTY

Hero did go once to Andy to try and say that Andy should leave the steakhouse for a place where there were other kids. But even to himself, Hero's voice sounded as though it were coming up from under water, and by any appearance it did not affect Andy. It didn't seem that Andy was angry with Hero; there was only the familiar sense that Andy could have nothing to do with Hero because no one else had anything to do with Hero.

Maybe Hero's voice did not in fact reach the surface at all. Which would have made sense, because the figure that Hero had seen begin to emerge, his own shape, was gone again entirely.

The world was as it always had been, except for one new thing which Hero now did often and automatically, and which for that reason may not have counted for anything new at all.

There was a four-inch-square metal plate on an electrical outlet box at chest height beside the door out from the kitchen into the dining room. The plate was sprung a fraction of an inch from the outlet box, and you pressed the plate to open the door. It was at a height where if your hands were full, you could hit it with an elbow, or else back against it. The door stayed open just long enough so that once you hit the plate, there was time to put both hands on a guéridon and push the guéridon out the doorway into the dining room. In fact the plate did not demand hitting. Hero had been in the habit of pushing it with his fingertips as he went out. Most often with the fingertips of his left hand, since the plate was on the left side of the door. It was an automatic motion. There were countless passages out that door in the course of only one night. In a week, a month, several months, that automatic motion to the spring plate was as unconscious as breathing, on a day when there was no trouble breathing.

Now, however, Hero no longer pressed the spring plate with his fingertips. Now he gave little punches at the plate. Sometimes with only his left fist, sometimes with his right fist. Often he hit it twice, in a one-two. He led across his body with his right, a jab it would have been, because Hero was left-handed. Then he immediately followed that right with a short left. The plate was just there beside his left elbow, so Hero could simply lift and clench his fist and roll his shoulder to deliver that hit with the left hand. They were quick, light, unobtrusive taps, bing bing, not at all the sort of thing that anyone would notice in even someone as silent as Hero. Still, for Hero, there was a satisfaction in that casual succession of raps to the plate. With the rolled shoulder and the closeness of the plate and the possibility of leaning in behind the shoulder, there was also a sense that the left could be a real and damaging punch.

This was a restaurant in which almost all of the lunch customers were men. The majority of the customers at dinner were also men. The women who did come in to dinner were often the wives of the businessmen who came for lunch, and even if they were sometimes relatively young, they were not often either elegant or splendid to look at. On the weekends there were other sorts of both men and women that came through, but most often these were not on expense account, and were deplorable for that. Since the restaurant was an expensive one though, there were also now and then some fallen celebrities and even some true celebrities, maybe a basketball player or a boxer, a singer or a newscaster. Rarely, but it did happen, a beautiful woman would show up.

The gays would spot her first. Then the Mexican would notice, and he would go by the desk and point her out to Chick who would say, "I was in her pants an hour ago," unless he thought she was too good for the waiters, and then he would assume silent feudal possession. O'Meara didn't notice women unless he was well on with his Sambuca and there came one of the late, softening floozies from his own youth as a bartender.

All of this was nothing to Hero. Old or young, beautiful or terrifyingly ugly, whether appreciated by Castro the Cuban, Hussein the Iranian, or Chick the maître d' with his pressed tuxedo and crooked, unemployed model's smile. Hero might as well have considered for their appeal the black Olympic boxer favored by Robert and the suave advertising executive pampered by Henke. So, when on one night that Castro the Cuban was Hero's back man, and Castro discovered a beauty on their own station, Castro did not bother to announce it to Hero.

Castro announced it to the other waiters as they passed through the station, or else Castro went to their stations to tell them, or told them downstairs in the hot kitchen while waiting to pick up. The other waiters came one after another to look at Castro's beauty, but none of them came back for second looks or lascivious circling. The other waiters did not think Castro's beauty was beautiful.

Castro savored her by himself. Then when finally that was not enough, he did at last urge Hero to admire her. She had black hair and broad, flattened, Indian features. Her eyes were purpled and were heavy with eyelashes. Her mouth was large and darkly reddened, and she sat back against her banquette as if she had had enough to drink to make her comfortable. Because she sat back and because the table was wide and the tablecloth hung low, there was not much of her body to see.

"You had to see her walk in," Castro said. "A beautiful body. A beautiful body." It was what he said to all the other waiters.

"When she sat down, she buttoned the top button. You'll see. When she stands up. When she moves."

Castro said these things quite as though Hero would look when she got up at the end of her meal. Nor did Castro stop with her body. He said to Hero — there was no one else around — "I would love her even without the body. I love the face. I love her face, and if I weren't already married and have my two babies, I would follow her home and ask her to marry me. You know what I mean? Sometimes you love a face so much that it breaks your heart. It happens to me when I am drunk. But I am not drunk tonight. Just a couple of beers tonight."

Then Castro went off to get desserts for another table in the station. Hero did not look at the woman again until after Castro had cleared away her dinner and the dinner of her companion, an older woman.

As Hero came to the table to sell them desserts, Castro's woman put a hand to the side of her head. She twisted in her seat and she sat up straight to look down in the lap of her skirt and on the banquette beside herself. Her friend began to look as well.

Castro's beauty said to Hero, "My earring."

Hero looked quickly to see if Castro could be signaled back. Castro would want the chance to help her. Or else Hero was reluctant to get down on his hands and knees, which was unlikely.

But Castro was gone into the kitchen, and since it was nearly the end of the night and most tables had left, he might stay to bullshit with the other waiters in there.

"Please," the woman said. "Like this one," and she pulled off of her other ear a clip earring which was an irregular beaten shape in a dull, gold color.

Hero knelt down on the floor.

"Can you see it?" she called to him from above and behind the folds of the tablecloth.

He could not, but he stayed a minute longer on the floor so that she would know he had looked. The floor was not altogether clean, but it was free of jewelry. Then however she must have

twisted around to look behind herself on the banquette. Hero
saw her shoes and ankles turn about, and heard the rustling,
and there was the sound of something fallen to the floor.

"Yes," he said quickly. There it was, and he leaned over his
knees to reach it. His knees hurt.

The woman swept aside the long tablecloth, and slid to the
side on her banquette. There were her legs, to her knees, and
the black skirt around her knees, and she herself was bent down
over her knees to see Hero and her found earring. Her face was
hardly inches from Hero's face, and she smiled delightedly.
Hero was startled by her suddenness, and for an instant he simply looked back at her. Then, as if to be polite, he smiled back at
her smile, and she laughed. Hero flushed, and realized, looking
away from them, that she had pretty legs.

She slid forward and part way off of the banquette, toward
Hero, holding her hand out at his hand. In sliding forward, her
skirt slid back halfway up her thighs. Hero looked away from
that to her face, and still she smiled at him. Her free hand was
below her throat, and she unbuttoned the two top buttons to her
red embroidered blouse, and the blouse opened enough for
Hero to see, almost to touch with his breath, her two very full
breasts swelling against the white, laced cups inside the blouse.

Her extended hand closed around Hero's hand. He had forgotten to let go of her earring. He knew that now but he did not
now let go. He saw her breasts and the pleasure in her face, and
felt her hand on his own hand, and he was confused as to where
this was happening. Then he did open his hand, and she took
back the ring, and he rocked away on his heels. He fell almost
over backward, and had to brace his other hand behind himself
quickly. He struggled in a flurry to get to his feet rather than go
prone across the floor of his station. On his feet, he was dizzy,
and he heard the woman say, "Thank you," but he did not look.
He was dizzy and he nodded and he slapped with his palms at
the dust on his black trousers. He went to the busing stand and
looked at the stack of ashtrays. Castro was back, and Hero asked
him to take a dessert order from the two women, and Castro was

happy to do that. The beauty was leaned against her banquette again and talking with her partner. Her blouse was buttoned fully up, and her legs were behind the tablecloth.

"Waiter?"

This was aimed at Hero from the single in the corner, an old woman on the only other table Hero had left. Since the vacancy which occupied him at the end of a night was not yet filling into him, Hero went gratefully to the old woman on that single in the corner. She had refused dessert and had now a full pot of hot coffee. Maybe she wanted an after-dinner drink, though she did not look it. She was old; that was what struck Hero. Old as Hero. If Hero were to be matched ever again with a woman, it would be with a woman as old as this one, which for some reason was comforting.

He stood before her with his hands at his sides, and bent at the waist. "May I bring something else?"

The woman seemed in need, but Hero had to wait for her to speak.

She shook her head. "I'm sorry," she said. She was embarrassed and she smiled awkwardly.

"Will you have an after dinner-drink?"

"I'm sorry," the woman said again, and lost her smile. Into the air above the table, she said quietly, "I am an old woman."

"That's all right. I'm an old man."

Hero was appalled to hear himself say that, and to hear the intimate tone in which it was said. He stood up straight and began to back away.

"Thank you," the woman said, and she had her awkward smile, and she had a look as strangely intimate as Hero was afraid his own voice had been.

He went to the busing stand and put his hands flat on its linen cover. He could stand idle. He could begin turning into the silence he would become when his shift was over. He could anticipate stiffness in his knees turning sore as he went down the stairs to the hot kitchen, could smell the breath of the toilet along the hall to the lockers. Beyond the gloss of the toilet's overflow was the shine of garbage waiting to be baled, and beyond that the dark gap into the lockers. Over garbage and baler stood the iron stair to the service street door, but the fact of silence came before that. It was once he was past the toilet that Hero was altogether gone from every customer, from any need to speak or be spoken to, away already into the success which had once been simply a roof over his head but now was a decades-sober numbness as safe as death.

Hero put a hand into his pocket to touch at his keys, and with his other hand felt the silt of crumbs on the linen cover of his busing stand. He let the silence at the end of the night gather him. He was ready to go. And ready to return again past the toilet for the next service.

In place of gathering silence, however, the sound of his own voice went in his head like a wooden unround ball, saying, "I'm an old man." Was he? The word, "I'm" rang against metalled walls. I'm, I'm, I'm, and the ether in which the reverberation moved was scented not with basement departure, but with the intimacy which had been so intrusive in Hero's voice, and in the woman's look. Why should she thank him?

The dining room was large and high ceilinged and a smooth, pale, well-lighted color of sand. It was nearly square, but the several broad posts to the ceiling, and the alcoved screen of deuces at one end, broke up the squareness, and the dark bank of the leather-backed banquettes all around the walls gave a second tone to the color of the walls as though from paneling. At the front corner were the steps up to the bar, which ran toward the customers' street door. Now, at the table nearest the end of the bar, O'Meara sat with a water glass of Sambuca and the night's checks.

Castro parked his guéridon beside their own station's busing stand, and stood next to Hero to watch their beautiful woman. From this parking place, Castro had a vantage that was to the side and a bit behind, so the woman would not notice his stare.

"Beautiful, beautiful, beautiful," Castro said aloud to himself.

Without a thought for whether it was a sensible thing to say, Hero said, "Yes," and felt no surprise he had said it.

Castro leaned to him so that their shoulders were touching. "Yes?" Castro said. "You think so, too?"

Hero had no idea what he thought, but he looked at the back of her head and the profile of her cheekbone, and he said to Castro, "She is beautiful."

Castro looked with Hero and said, "Her face too. I love that."

Hero said to the back of her head, "Everything." To Castro he said, "You should marry her."

"Hah." Castro laughed one triumphant noise, and then laughed again softly and wistfully. He shook his head. "A woman like that for me, for Castro? I am afraid not." But then he hit his fist on the busing stand. He looked hard at Hero and then harder still at the back and side of the beautiful woman's head. "Yes," Castro said. "I will marry her. A man should have two wives. This man, I, Castro, must have two. I am going to ask her right now. I will take her to my bed tonight. My other wife, for tonight, can sleep with the babies."

Castro looked away. "Oh oh," he said to Hero. "The old one wants you again."

Hero pulled the old woman's check and closed it in the folder and went and set it down for her. He would have turned away, but the woman spoke too quickly.

"I wanted," she said, almost urgently, as if to catch and hold him at the table, "I wanted to explain why I called at you before. You looked so much to me the way some of the young men I knew would have grown to look. That must sound peculiar, but I find suddenly that I am saying peculiar things almost daily. Forgive me. I didn't mean to intrude. They were good-looking young men, I thought, at the time."

Hero looked to the right of her shoulder, and tilted himself a bit toward her so that it would appear, if she wanted, that he was listening.

"Please," she said, and there was such discouragement in her voice that the voice had gone cold, "Forgive me." Hero left her with the check.

Castro was pulling the table out for the other two, the beautiful woman and her companion. Hero stood back from them so that Castro might be the one to usher them out and to say good-bye to his woman. But that beautiful young woman looked past Castro, and came the few steps out of her way over to Hero. She took Hero's hand, and standing close to Hero, as tall as he was, or more, she said, "Thank you for finding my earring." Then she laughed, and there was such pleasure in her face, such fun, that Hero too made something like a laugh. She turned and walked toward the bar and the way out, going quickly to catch up with her companion.

Castro was right. She was voluptuous. She walked away like a cresting swell, thighs and buttocks, broad back and heavy breasts. Hero could not take his eyes from her, or from the spot were she turned out of sight down the bar.

Castro hit him on the shoulder with an open palm. "She liked you," Castro hissed. "She liked you, Man. My first night of marriage and you stole her. I promise a broken beer bottle in your face. My beautiful bride, and you stole her."

The other waiters, scattered among the tables, were all just now also finished looking after Castro's beautiful woman. The Bolivian looked to Castro and made a movement with his fist and his forearm, and Castro whispered loudly in the near empty dining room for Fedy Llosa and for the others as well, "You didn't believe me. I told you. Beautiful. She was beautiful," and Castro laughed and rolled his guéridon to the emptied table to clear and reset.

The elderly woman was up from her table, and Hero made a quick half-step toward her to show that he had meant to pull her table away for her. He also made a slight bow so he would not have to look at her, but she stopped beside him. "I think you must be a nice man," she said. "The young men I knew were not always altogether nice." She said it softly, so that when she was done there was no sense that she had finished. She hesitated a moment longer and then said, "Good-bye." Hero stood up from his bow, but he still did not meet her eyes. He smiled for her the smile of someone in another universe, the smile of an old waiter alone at the end of a shift and absolutely separate from every other human being. Most especially separate from anyone that might eat where he served. He noticed as she went up the steps to the bar and her way out that she held to the bannister, and that her old legs were stiff and fleshless.

WEDNESDAY NIGHTS

"What do you think?" Fedy Llosa said, to none of them in particular and to all of them. "You think Hero is gay?"

Hero was against the kitchen wall in the hour before service. He sat straight backed on an empty glass-rack, with his legs square in front of him, his arms straight, and his hands on his knees. It was a stable position of balance, and he looked between his knees to the floor. Among the other waiters the Polack had a Polish paper from his sister in Buffalo. Castro the Cuban was asleep with his head back on the counter of the warming cabinet and with an aluminum bowl propped over his face. Hussein the Iranian stood studying the schedules, which were kept posted on the wall opposite the bread warmer, there between the door in from the dining room and the door out to the dining room.

Actually Hussein, along with the Mexican, the Frenchman, and Bogart the Chinese, was one of the waiters with good, fixed nights, but Hussein liked to study the schedules for the changes to which the other waiters were always liable. The good nights in the restaurant were Monday through Thursday, with Tuesday and Thursday better than Monday, and with Wednesday nights the best. Hussein had all the good nights, and took Sunday for his fifth night, because Sunday was so bad that he often got to go home early. Friday and Saturday nights, on the other

hand, the restaurant stayed open an extra hour and could sometimes be flooded with cheap, difficult customers. On Friday and
Saturday nights all the gays worked along with Fedy Llosa the
Bolivian and with the newest waiters, both the green ones and
the ones who knew as soon as they were hired how to rip off
booze and food and sometimes clothes from the lockers downstairs in the pit. At the end of every Saturday night, as he moved
through his third glass of Sambuca, O'Meara produced the
schedule for the next week, and the waiters then clustered
between the doors in the kitchen to see what they had, and to
complain or gloat, or to appraise someone else's improvement or
dismay.

"I think he is," Fedy Llosa called. "I think Hero is gay as
Robert."

This was a quiet Sunday night, and there was no reaction
among the rest of the waiters.

"Who did I see you with last night? Downstairs in the toilet."

The Bolivian himself did not have his heart in it. He was idle
and his eyes were hooded in drowsiness. He appeared to be
hibernating with animal contentment. And yet one ganglion of
manic nerve still floated about him, ready for arousal. So when
it had been quiet long enough again that there would be no
sense of cause and effect, Hero got up to go to the dining room.
To get there he had to pass the Iranian who was still studying
the schedules between the dining room doors.

Hussein didn't see the new schedule on Saturday with everyone else, and when he did see it, he took his time with it; he
checked it back against the previous week's schedule which was
always left up a week past its use. Lately, he had also wanted to
instruct Hero on how the schedule worked. He had been able
early to spot Hero's acceptance into the restaurant's establish-
ment, because Hero had been given steady nights right away,
and when Hero was worked into a couple of midweek nights, it
was not at the expense of one of the established waiters. Those
early schedules had long since been torn down, but Hussein
could recall clearly that they had fed Hero into spots occupied

by waiters who were new themselves or who were weak and unpopular. It was Hussein's contention now that soon Hero would get a Wednesday.

"Look," Hussein said, and intercepted Hero's path to the dining room. He had a finger on Andy's name in the past week's schedule, and a finger on Andy's name in the current schedule. Andy's schedule was the same for both weeks, the four worst nights.

"He's not going to make it," Hussein said. "You know that; I know that; even Chick knows it. O'Meara should have gotten rid of him this week." Now with the finger of just one hand, Hussein rapped back and forth to Andy's name this week and Andy's name last week. "You know what's happening? Andy is so bad they can even keep him past the union cutoff. They are saving Andy for the Frenchman, to have a little fun. Which is why the cooks saw Fat Tom last week."

From the guéridons, Fedy Llosa spoke once more, a little louder but no more eagerly. "I think it was with the Camel Driver that I saw Hero in the toilet. Old camel for the old Camel Driver."

"Go fuck yourself, Bolivian scum," Hussein yelled back without taking his finger off Andy.

To Hero again, the Iranian said, "They keep that insane Bolivian just because he is insane. His insanity among the rest of us makes the managers holy. It is true. Llosa the Bolivian is our proof that Chick and O'Meara and Fat Tom are God. But the Frenchman, the Frenchman is getting too slow. The Frenchman is not as old as you and I, but he can't keep up anymore, so they are going to squeeze him out, with Andy. If Andy doesn't do the job, they can always put the Frenchman in back, behind the Bolivian, and get it over with quick. And then who knows, maybe they try Andy on somebody else before they put him out. Yes, this Andy makes a change; he is fun for them. I have seen it before. When we get too old, they will do it to us. The Frenchman will not be able to catch on at a new place, but his wife died this year; he had insurance."

Hero shook his head and moved to go on past, but the Iranian held out an arm to keep him at the schedules.

"You'll see. I have told the Frenchman, but the Frenchman will walk only in his own private mud. When he is enough stuck in that mud, he will ask them to shoot him. And with his last breath he will curse me for not having such fine mud as he has. All of the French arrogance and none of the cunning. He keeps his towel over his arm, and his precious accent sounds like Long Island. He will not last much more."

"I'll get his Wednesday nights," Hero said.

"That's right. You get the Wednesdays as soon as they send the Frenchman to die on Long Island. Maybe first they ask you to push Andy into the river. You see how smart you get if you listen to Hussein? Or you knew all along. Maybe you've been watching the Frenchman's Wednesday night since you got here."

Hussein turned back toward the guéridons and shouted, "Hey, Bolivian with the damaged brain. I am talking here to an intelligent man. When you get your intelligence repaired, you come talk with us." Fedy Llosa had put his large head down on one of the guéridons though, and did not move.

Hussein said to Hero, "You are thinking that it might be merciful to trip him. To take all the dinner checks he cannot remember anymore to put back in his pocket. We can do it on the next busy night when he is stuck and his checks are left on the desserts. Where should we hide them? Then he cannot find the checks, and all his customers scream, and the kitchen downstairs screams, and O'Meara and Chick watch him drown. The Frenchman knows it is coming. Will he cry like a baby? Will he drop his towel? Maybe he will go out into the street in his white coat with his towel over his arm and try to walk to his empty home in Long Island without turning his head. He is run over on Lexington in front of Bloomingdale's. Then you take the Wednesdays. Maybe we don't even need Andy after all."

"I'm sorry," Hero said, and again moved to go on to the door for the dining room. Again Hussein held him where he was.

"Sorry for what? You are one of us, Hero. They don't want you sorry. They like you with your mouth shut and with you watching out for your Wednesday. The Frenchman cannot do the work anymore. Take your Wednesday and make some money so your kids can afford to bury you."

Hussein paused, and studied Hero. Then he said, "How many kids do you have, Hero?"

Hero did not answer him.

"So keep the money from your Wednesday nights. Spend it. Live forever. I am going to live forever. You and I will bury Chick and O'Meara. We will live until there are two Wednesdays in the week. We will even bury Fat Tom the invisible motherfucking general manager, because it is Fat Tom who tells O'Meara what to do. O'Meara, when he was a bartender, never even invented a drink. We'll bury them all, but you know what will never change? No. Don't look at the dining room door. Answer me."

"The schedule," Hero said.

"The schedule," Hussein said. "You want to be my friend, don't be so smart. When I was a young man, I studied schedules so that all the ones in my country like these motherfuckers here could have better lives. I wanted to make a better schedule. I spent my youth at it. If I were not going to live forever I would say I spent also my middle age, getting knowledge of how the rulers did what they did in my country. Now that I am a waiter here and as old as you, I know it does not matter, either here or in my country, how the rulers do. It matters if these motherfuckers can get their Wednesday night. Ask them. And if these ever get to be the rulers, then the next motherfuckers after these ones all will want the Wednesday nights. And you and I too, Hero. It doesn't do any good to pretend to be stupid so someone truly stupid can have your Wednesday night. Out there on the floor is the Frenchman standing in his station with his towel over his arm pretending he is still a waiter, pretending that when the customers come there will not be too many for him and he will not get stuck again. He pretends O'Meara and

Chick have not yet told Fat Tom. He is sorry it has to be him the Frenchman that will be squeezed out. He thinks he looks too much like a Frenchman and a waiter to get squeezed out."

"He's not fair with his back men."

"He cheats his back man and he doesn't tip the bartender and he is rude to the Haitian salad man over here. So nobody helps him. He is stupid and arrogant, and if he could feed me to the schedule, he would. That's what I learn from studying politics."

"Why did they give him the good nights?"

"No Frenchman worth a damn works in a steakhouse, especially with an Iranian. And I am the best of the others here. They wanted a Frenchman, and he was the only Frenchman they could get. You think the mangers are smart? If they were smart, then we would become smart. They are stupid, and they give us the chance to eat one another. For what more could we ask?"

"I won't take his Wednesday."

"Who are you not to take? You're one of us. You have to. Only you are too quiet and gentle. That's why they work you in and why they give you finally the good nights. You are a good waiter too, but that is not so important to them as that they think they know who you are and what they can do with you. You are one of the easy ones for them. But once you have the good nights, then all these in here will want to take it away from you. The Frenchman cannot change, so it is just as well for him not to listen. But if you can become tough, then you should do it. All these motherfuckers will look at you and they will say that you are not tough enough to keep that Wednesday night."

Hero shook his head.

"Yes. Look at them."

"Why are you telling me?"

"I told the Frenchman because I hate him, and if I didn't tell him, then I would be guilty of helping to push him in the street. My conscience is sick, but I cannot kill it, so I tell the Frenchman and then I look another way when he goes under the third time."

"But why are you telling me, Hussein?"

"What's the matter with you? I like you. I don't want them to eat you. I want to keep you here for someone to talk to. You are intelligent. Maybe that's what happened in your other restaurants before you came here — people discovered you. Right? You think you are invisible. To these others for now you are invisible, but not to me. And not to them for much longer."

"Thank you," Hero said.

"Don't thank me. Tell me a joke. Become tougher."

"I'll try to help you, if you need it."

"I don't need it. I will help you, but I can only do so much. Watch the schedule. Watch the Frenchman and Andy. It's getting late, and the pigs are arriving. We must go out to feed the pigs. We are the lucky ones. We get to feed them on the nights when they are hungriest."

"I think he is," Fedy Llosa called. "I think Hero is gay."

"You hear them?" Hussein said. "They begin already to smell your Wednesday night. I study it and I understand it, but they smell it just as fast as I learn it. They cannot stop what they have to do."

STAND UP STRAIGHT

How many kids do you have? Hero could not imagine an answer to that. He could not imagine anyone asking.

It was another night and he stood at the service end of the bar to cash out what credit card tips he had so far. It had been busy early, and good. The barman counted over a hundred and forty-five and Hero thanked him. If the expensive four-top were good, Hero and Castro would make a hundred each tonight.

He saw the elderly woman standing alone at the desk.

There were no more reservations, and Chick was downstairs in the office, and O'Meara had sat down at his table to eat and begin collecting checks. O'Meara sensed her though, and shifted as if he would get up.

The waiters on the floor had sensed her too, had seen her, and were turning their backs, willing her away from their stations. They, as Hero, had all made good early money, and you could see it in their closing shoulders, "Not here, not here."

It was only two or three paces for Hero, so he reached her before O'Meara. "Will you sit with me again this evening?"

The woman was waiting for O'Meara to struggle around from his table and come to her, so she was startled by Hero.

She said, "Hello," and as she said it, she recognized him from her dinner at his table once before, from the night of Castro's beauty. She began a distant smile.

"You want her, Hero?" O'Meara said.

Both the woman and Hero were now surprised by O'Meara, or by what he'd asked. Enough surprised that there was a moment before Hero had the sense to answer.

In that moment the woman was obliged to watch Hero, and wonder what he would say.

"Yes," he said.

It was nothing to O'Meara, who turned again and lumped back down the three steps to his table and his dinner.

The woman, however, was made shy. She was elderly, and simply dressed, but she had a firm, erect posture and she had finely boned features. She was a lady. She was also pretty, or her sudden unlikely shyness made her seem so. Hero had spoken for her, and it actually passed through his mind that she was waiting for him to take her hand.

He bowed and said, "Please."

He was so intent on not looking at her that he found himself looking Castro in the eye. Castro, who was his back man again tonight, his back man regularly now, had come up to wish on behalf of their station that the woman not be given to them. Castro saw and understood, put both hands on top of his head. Hero went, firmly, down the three steps to the dining room floor, and led the woman back at the station and back in fact to the table in the corner where she had sat before. Hero did not look again at Castro. He would give Castro an extra twenty. He worried what he would say to the woman once he had seated her.

When he'd pulled the table for her, and given her a menu, she looked, not helpless, but as if she needed something else, something easy, something which she ordinarily would have. She looked pleasantly perturbed by her lack. She appeared to Hero to be someone he would be lucky to be able to help, and he stood by her table after he had given the menu, and he said, "What?"

She was not looking at the menu, and neither had she said anything. What was Hero asking her? She seemed to know. A brightness came to her face as though she'd now remembered, and she said, "Is it Hero that they call you?"

He did not like to be called by name, so he was not a waiter who gave his name to customers, but this woman asked nicely, and still shyly, and Hero said, "Yes."

"I heard the other man say it, and I thought what a fine name, and then just now I altogether forgot it when I wanted to remark upon it. May I call you Hero?"

Hero shrugged and nodded.

"I'm Molly," she said. "I'd be very happy to have somebody call me Molly."

Hero nodded again and backed away, so that she would pick up her menu. He needed to close the checks on his last two fours. He asked Castro to take the order from the woman.

"See?" Castro said. "Everybody else is going home. I give her thirty seconds to look at the menu. Everything is rare."

Then immediately Castro was back because Hero had neglected to give him the dupe pad. "Once we get her started," Hero said, "you can go. We'll split her tip tomorrow."

"You think O'Meara and Chick want Castro to go when they have to stay? Okay. She gets another minute. I am counting. Does this mean that you give me back my beauty you stole? Now that this old one comes back for you? Or you are keeping both of them? This one is old enough to know all the tricks, but my woman was beautiful. My heart is still broken. Forty seconds more. I brought those another mousse. Put another mousse on this check. They can afford it. Sons of bitches."

In a moment again he was back. "She wants you. She is taking her pants off, and she doesn't want Castro. And Castro doesn't want her. You can tell her I said so. I want back my own you took from me. And remember what I said. Everything is rare. We are going home early. Did we make a bill tonight?"

"I think so. We will for sure, with her tip."

"Then I am happier. I am an American. She can have medium rare."

Hero gave Castro the checks for the fours, and went to the woman, who looked as she had when she first sat down. Comfortable, almost pleased, but with a vague peripheral confusion.

"Thank you," she said when Hero reached her. "I'm afraid I wasn't prepared for your colleague." She was actually more unsettled now than she had been. "I've been at the hospital all day and I've lost my bearings somewhat and you seem so kind that I am hoping you will help me. I'm sure I know your name, and I've forgotten it. But I can see that I've come late to the restaurant. Do you think it is too late? Will you tell me if it is?"

"My name is Hero," he said, quietly to calm her.

"I'm Molly Crawford, Hero. Have I already told you that? I've had what seems like an endless day, and I . . . Will you tell me what you think I should have? I'm not very hungry, and I would like something quick so that you all can get home. Am I rude to call you Hero? I don't mean to be too friendly in that awful way."

"We have a small sirloin," Hero said, as quietly and as gently as he could to the woman. As he spoke she closed her eyes, but stayed erect and kept her soft, determined smile. "And we have salmon which I could bring plain if you'd like."

"I'll have the steak," she said, with her eyes open and her voice alert and decisive. "I wanted to come sit in a steakhouse, after all."

"How would you like it cooked?"

"You tell me, please. What's convenient? I'm at your mercy."

"My partner says you can have it rare. If you're a good tipper, medium rare." This too, Hero said gently.

She laughed immediately, and the laugh was such relief in her face that Hero was happy at what he had said.

"Tell him I want it well done," she said, still bright with her laughter. "And tell him not to start cooking it for half an hour while I relax." She grinned at Hero as if they'd been wonderfully clever together.

Hero smiled with her, and wrote in the dupe pad, and as he turned to give the dupes to Castro, she called to catch him.

"I didn't really . . ." and the worry was back to her voice, the gaiety gone from her smile.

Hero nodded and smiled, and held one finger to his lips. Castro was standing by the busing stand, where Hero gave him the dupes.

Castro glanced at the dupes, turned his back to the woman, spread his legs, and looked at the high ceiling. He took two straddling steps forward into the busing stand so he could set his round stomach out against the edge of the top of the stand. He took a step back from there and slapped a hand to his stomach and the hand stayed there. Still looking at the distant ceiling, Castro held the dupes toward Hero and said, as quietly as Hero had been speaking to the woman, "Well done? Holy fucking Mother of Teresa and all the starving babies in India."

Hero took the dupes from Castro, marked them to medium rare, and gave them back.

"That's better," Castro said, and turned for the kitchen, and turned back to Hero. "Wait a minute," Castro said. "That was a joke." Castro looked around. The Iranian was closest, and Castro went at him, talking freely because the dining room was emptying. "Hey," Castro said. "Hero made a joke."

Hero stood with his hands at his sides.

"Nah," Hussein said. "Hero? That motherfucker over there with no hair?"

Hero turned away from them.

"I told you," Castro said, and both Castro and Hussein laughed, and Hero felt a flush come to his face, and now Castro did go for the kitchen with the order, and Hussein turned to tell the Pole. Both fours needed coffee, and Hero did that.

Then Hero went in and got a salad from Aids, though the woman had not asked for a salad.

"Thank you," she said. "I'd forgotten I'd asked for one."

"You didn't, but it will take a few minutes for the steak, so I brought one anyway."

"I'd love a salad."

"It's on the house."

"No. Don't be silly."

"It's no trouble."

"I wouldn't dream of not paying for it. Besides, I wanted you to order for me."

Hero leaned to her so that she would understand. "I wanted to give you something."

She looked at him.

"I mean," he said, "that it's all right this late. At the end of the night they let us give away a salad. They..."

"Don't say that. I like it that you've given me something. I was right that you're a kind man. You have made me comfortable, and I see your friends laughing with you, and now you have brought me this salad. I know the restaurant doesn't give them away. I won't tell."

"Watch it, Boss." Castro rolled the guéridon then up beside the table.

"And here's my steak already," the woman said. "An embarrassment of riches."

Hero looked at Castro, but Castro would not look back. Castro said to the woman, as he moved her salad to one side and set down a steak knife and then the plate, "I saw you come in, Madam, and I said to myself, there is a lady who will have a small of the sirloin steak done to medium rare. I was so sure, I told the chef to begin cooking immediately. You see? In America everyone is happy. Enjoy your dinner, Madam. Take your time."

Hero reached for the plate. "We'll bring it to you when you're done with your salad."

"I won't hear of that," she said. "I always eat my salad with my meal." She put both hands to her plate, and she said to Castro. "Thank you so much. I'm starving. You couldn't have brought it soon enough."

"You're welcome, Madam," Castro said. "Since I have come to this country I have tried to do my best always." Castro backed off to park the guéridon by the busing stand, and the woman picked up her knife and fork, and so Hero had to come away also. Castro waited at the stand.

"What are you doing?" Hero said.

Castro stroked his stomach like it was a fed cat.

"What the hell were you doing?" Hero said more loudly.

"If she'd wanted the salmon," Castro said, "then there would have been no more salmon. Now she is happy, and we go early. But where did the salad come from? No salad is on the dupe."

"I gave her the salad."

"Then we are partners. You gave her the salad; I gave her the fast steak. At least I did not try to steal her. I gave to her and came away. That is a gentleman. Look: *dinero*."

Both parties of four had credit cards out, and Hero ran those through, and the people signed and were gone. When Hero and Castro had cleared and reset the tables, Castro followed Hero to the bar to watch the tips. It was sixty on the good four, so they had made their hundred each.

"We made the bill?" Castro said.

"More," Hero said.

"You see what happens when you work with a good waiter? Stick with me, and you are going to like it in America."

As Hero collected on the slips from the barman, the Chinese waiter Bogart, who with Andy had the only other party in the restaurant, lined up behind Hero and Castro, and Castro said, "You hear that tonight my partner made a joke? I swear it with both feet on my mother's grave."

Bogart said, "So?"

Castro said, "And you know what else he said to me, right now? He asked me, Castro, what the hell was I doing. Because he made a joke, suddenly he is going to talk like the Camel Driver."

"So, what the fuck did you do this time?" Bogart said.

"Oh yeah?" Castro said. He straightened up and put his hands on his stomach. "We made a bill tonight. You make a bill?"

"I always make a bill," Bogart said.

Hero folded their money, and Castro said to Bogart, "Oh yeah? So? We made our bill easy."

As Hero went down the steps and back at the station, Bogart said, "Your partner made a bill, Castro. You got your bill because you were in the right place."

The woman was alone in the station now, and had eaten some of her salad and much of her steak. She set down her knife and fork and looked at Hero, and he went to her.

"Is everything all right?"

"It's perfect. I've done all I can do, though. I hope you won't be upset if I don't finish."

"I never even found out how you really like your meat to be done."

"It was exactly right."

"I can wrap it up, if you'd like to take it home."

"Oh. I'm only visiting, and living half out of a suitcase. But yes. I can't sleep in hotels anymore, so a steak will give me something to do when I wake in the night."

"But not the salad?" Hero said it, and heard himself flirting.

"Not the salad," she said, and smiled. "Though I liked the salad best. Just the steak and the check, and then you both can go. Your partner will not be so upset with you."

"He's not really upset."

"He was upset that you wanted me in the first place."

For her to say that made Hero shy, as shy as she had been when O'Meara first asked whether Hero wanted her. She smiled quite boldly as Hero took her plate and went away to the kitchen.

He wrapped the steak and totaled the check, and when he came back she had cash ready. He went to the bar for change, and Castro said, "She is tax free, too. I begin to see why you love her. My beauty would not use money ever. My own beauty would put me into a higher bracket than with the babies I could afford."

The woman was up from the table when Hero got back with her change, and she put a tip to the table quickly and said, "Thank you," and smiled to Hero and stepped past him.

Castro stood by the stand with his hands on his stomach. He was bouncing from the pleasure of getting out early, or not as late as he feared, with good money. The woman said to Castro, "Did you see? I went as fast as I could."

"You were as fast as the wind, Madam. Only in America would a lady eat like that so a worker could go home early to his babies."

"Oh," she said. "How old are your babies?"

"They are three-and-a-half and six-and-a-half, and the teacher of the six-and-a-half has just given me a paper saying that one is the smartest in the class. So tonight I go home early to tell them good night, and I bring them a bill too."

"What's a bill?"

"A bill is a hundred dollars, Madam. American money."

"I'm sure you deserve it. Thank you."

"You're welcome. I would like to give you this." Castro had become drunk with his bill and his early leaving, or he had been taking more than his usual brandy from the cart. In one motion he pulled off his brown, restaurant clip-on, and held it at the woman.

The woman looked at the thing before her, and laughed. "I love a bow tie," she said. "But that is not my shade of brown."

Castro snapped it back on. "Then I will think of you whenever I wear it.

She laughed again, said good night again, and started away. And Hero saw that she'd left a fifty dollar bill on the table. Castro looked and saw it too, and Castro threw up his arms exultantly as if for a touchdown or a heavyweight championship. Hero grabbed the fifty and moved as quickly as he could to catch her. She had only gone a few paces. Castro dropped his hands to the top of his head.

"Madam," Hero said, taking from his pocket the night's tips to make change for her. Two twenties. He would keep ten. Even that was too much. She had stopped and turned to him, and she smiled at him fiddling with his money. "You left far too much," he said.

When he'd said that, and pulled his two twenties clear for her, she said, "I don't know anyone by that name," and she turned away again, toward the steps up to the end of the bar and the desk and the way out to the street. She was old, but she was erect. She was a lady. She had a stride. They were not high heels, but there were heels to her shoes, and she had a bounce. Hero stood in the middle of the floor holding all his money like a vendor. He watched her go, and couldn't think what to do with himself. He admired her walking. She was thin. He was the fat one, if anyone was.

"Molly," he called.

He called it quite out loud, because she was to the steps. She stepped up one of them, and waited for Hero as he came to her with all his money. He put the big roll back in his pocket. O'Meara sat at the table with a Sambuca and the checks, and stared at him. Chick was back to the desk and was muffling some sort of television laugh at Hero. Hero held the two twenties to her and stood a half head below her at the steps. He was out of breath, though he had not come farther than half across the floor. "Please," he said.

"Yes?" she said. She was satisfied, with Hero and with herself. She stood with her hands at her sides and waited for whatever Hero would ask.

"Take these," Hero said, and held the twenties to her. "Even ten is too much," he said.

"All right," she said, and she took the bills from him. "But I knew what I was leaving, and I did accept your salad, and so you're not being fair."

"Thank you," Hero said.

"Thank you." She walked away down the bar for the coat room and the street door.

When she passed an unmarked point, beyond which she was closer to the coat room and the street than the desk, O'Meara and Chick both began at once a mimicking of Hero's call. "Mmmaahhhleee."

Chick only gave it his usual derogation, but for O'Meara the call was a first effort to express amazement.

"Hero?" O'Meara said. "Is that really you? Did you know her? Are you drunk, Hero?"

With Castro in the station and with only Bogart and Andy still working a table, back in the far corner of the room, no other waiters were near. The barman was at the other end of the bar checking those bottles. It was Chick at the desk and O'Meara sitting at his table with all the dinner checks and his Sambuca and with his tie loosened. Hero stood at the foot of the steps, all the light, high-ceilinged, leather-backed, white-clothed dining room behind him, as the woman, in a heavy, handsome wool coat, returned. Hero watched her, and Chick turned to her. O'Meara, from where he sat, could not see her, but must have heard her heels on the parquet through the empty bar.

She came to Chick. She brought Chick the two twenty dollar bills. She handed them to him, and she smiled a far more patrician smile than she had had for Hero, and she said from a distinguished altitude of wealth and breeding, "I'd like you and the other man in charge of the dining room each to have one of these. I had a delightful dinner. Thank you so much. I am Mrs. Crawford and I will be back."

Chick took the two twenties with polished solicitation. "Mrs. Crawford. Thank you. We were . . ."

She stepped away from him to the top of the three steps down to the dining room, to above where Hero stood. "Good night," she said to him in the voice of a friend, and with a simple smile altogether different from what she had for Chick. When she'd said that, "Good night," then she said, by itself, "Hero."

And smiled again and left for good. Hero again saw her flaunting her stride. He was also aware that O'Meara had been leaning on his stomach up over his table to get a look at her. Chick came down and handed one of the twenties to O'Meara.

"I take it all back, Hero," Chick said. "Whatever I was going to say, I eat. Mrs. Crawford is charming."

At the station, Castro waited.

"How much?"

"Forty."

"*Oye, Maria. Quarenta.* And all to Chick and Sambuca Gordo?"

Hero nodded.

"Hieyy."

"I'll give you an extra twenty. I was going to anyway. Because I took her in the first place."

"No. You are in love. Besides, I tried to win her from you with my bow tie, and that was shameful. Did we still make our bill?"

"Fifteen extra."

"I feel better. Your woman loves you, and I cannot steal her. When I love a woman, she betrays me. Still, it is easier for me to go home to the old wife and babies when I go with money. With money in America, anything can happen. Maybe tomorrow the second wife, and the second car, both."

While Castro talked Hero divided up the money. Castro put his in his pocket and headed for the kitchen to go downstairs and back to the pit to change for his bus home.

After checking the station, Hero followed.

Bogart and Andy still had seven people on the raised table between the kitchen doors. Bogart would have made a point of staying late for a party of seven, especially during the week. It was a very good deal to work with Bogart because Bogart always had the tables and always made money, and Andy was Bogart's back man tonight because Eddie Loo, Bogart's regular back man, was out suddenly with a streak in Atlantic City.

Now Andy had his guéridon loaded with dinner plates from the seven, and stood ready to push through into the kitchen. The plates were not well balanced on the guéridon, and Bogart was selling desserts and brandies, so Hero hesitated. He nodded to Andy, and then shuffled some of the plates into steadiness, pulled and gathered some of the silver, laid the glasses. He would then have moved along beside, to hold it all on, as Andy pushed into the kitchen. He was glad that Andy had had a night with Bogart and made some money.

But Andy did not push the guéridon into the kitchen. Andy was careless from the prospect of all the money Bogart was making for him, and he had found on one of the plates a nice piece of steak which apparently was not to be wrapped and taken. In every restaurant the waiters ate food from the plates, but Andy, right there beside the seven, picked up a piece of meat the size of a pint bottle of whiskey and held it out between himself and Hero. He smiled as if to boast what he had and Hero did not.

Andy put the thing to his mouth and, grinning, ripped off a bite.

Hero grabbed the guéridon and shoved it at the door, and grabbed Andy's sleeve to jerk him after. The kitchen door swung open and the stacks of ill-piled plates rattled going through, but did not fall. Andy followed, smiling around his wad of meat that he held to his face now as if it were membership in his new career.

Once inside the kitchen, Hero shoved the guéridon to the counter for Andy to unload it, and shoved it hard enough that two of the plates did slide off, one shattering.

Except for the Chinese dishwashers behind the counter, and Aids cleaning up his salads and desserts, the kitchen was empty. Everyone else had long since gotten their early money and gone.

Hero hit the steak away from Andy's face so hard that the meat slapped over against the coffee machines, and then banged to the drip grate. "What's the matter with you, you stupid son of a bitch?" Hero shouted this at Andy and kept on shouting, as Bogart came in.

"Where do you think you are? Don't you have a brain in your God damned head? Eating off their plates right beside them? You stupid prick. Don't you get it? Wise up, for Christ sake. This is a restaurant. We work here. If you don't know what to do here, get the hell out. Get the fucking hell out of here."

Hero stopped, and Bogart said to Andy, much more quietly than Hero, "You ever do that again on a table of mine, and I'll kill you."

Andy stood with his forearms before him and his hands hanging. His glasses were loose on his nose, but he did not fix them.

"For God sake," Hero screamed. "Stand up straight and look like a man."

"You understand?" Bogart said quietly.

Andy looked at Bogart and put his hands down to his sides. Andy straightened himself and whispered, "Yes."

"Clean up your mess," Hero shouted. "You worthless little jerk." Hero was so frozen with fury that he could not walk away. He reached out in a swipe with his open hand to throw a pile of plates off the guéridon, but he missed, and only skipped off a wine glass which popped against the side of the counter. One of the dishwashers made an irritated shout and began splashing with the hose. Then Hero did turn and go, his shortness of breath tugging in his chest.

ADIEU

Hero found the dinner checks to all but one of the Frenchman's tables tucked between the box of American Express slips and the box of Master and Visa slips, to the side of the credit card machines. The machines and the slips were on a shelf at chest height above the bread warmer, and on a busy night there, people grabbed and threw bread, ran and confirmed cards, figured taxes and put totals to slips. It was understandable that the Frenchman would be closing one table's check, and set all his other checks to the side.

"Leave the checks," Bogart said.

Bogart stood beside Hero, waiting for an approval code on an American Express. He wrote another check while he waited. He did not look at Hero or at the neat batch of the Frenchman's checks standing almost hidden among the charge slips.

Bogart was American Chinese and his speech was quick and businesslike and absolutely authoritative. "He is through. He is driving away good customers. They have put him with Andy to finish him off."

The code came up, Bogart wrote it on his slip, pocketed his checks, and left.

Hero took the Frenchman's checks and went out on the floor to the Frenchman's station, where the Frenchman was putting down main courses for a party of five. The Frenchman served awkwardly, but with much formality. Andy was not to be seen, gone for a forgotten sauce or vegetable, so the Frenchman served alone. With each plate put down, he managed to reach across a customer, and swivel loose knives with the napkin dragging from his forearm. After each plate was on the table, he stood and patted his jacket and looked, without notice of missing silver or unopened potato, around the table. He fingered his napkin to a good line. He went back to the guéridon for the next plate, and at the guéridon had to study his dupe to see which plate went where.

Hero looked again for Andy, and then, to help, reached for a couple of plates.

The Frenchman concentrated so hard on his dupe and his guéridon and this problem of five people to be served that he was alarmed when Hero stepped at the guéridon and moved to take up the plates.

"Get away," the Frenchman said to Hero's hands, and actually made a pushing sort of punch at Hero's arm. He did not look at Hero's face. He seemed trying to keep his concentration on all the remaining plates; he took up one of them with both hands. Hero set the checks down on the guéridon's cloth next to the heavily penned printing of the back man's name, Andy's name. But before Hero could move off, a sound of distress gurgled from the Frenchman. After that noise, the Frenchman did lift his eyes to see who it was that had put the checks down. His eyes were wet with fear and regret, but he tried to make his mouth firm and to lift his cheeks and to push out his fallen chest. His hands fidgeted on the plate which he held as though he were holding the quieted steering wheel of a vehicle that had damaged a child.

"It's just me," Hero said. "They were on the shelf over the bread, between the charge slips."

The Frenchman registered some relief that it was only Hero, but his fingers continued to work on the plate, and his arms quivered. His eyes now darted between the plate, the checks, the plate; he could not understand in his confusion how to hold the plate with one hand and pick up the checks with the other. Hero reached for the plate, and the Frenchman pulled the plate in to himself. The customers at the table had turned to look for the rest of their dinners. Hero took up the checks from beside Andy's name, slipped them quickly into the side pocket of the Frenchman's jacket, and backed away. Chick, who had just seated a party on the front wall, was watching. Hero glanced to the desk, and there O'Meara was watching.

The two Chinese waiters, Bogart and his regular back man Eddie Loo, were ready to leave when Hero got downstairs and past the toilet, past the baler and the garbage to the doorway of the pit, as it was called, a high, narrow, brick room without a light. Damp dripped from the ceiling in wet weather, and sweated from the walls more often than that, and the waiters with their lockers at the far end kept candles there on a glass-rack. Hero wore his black work pants, black work shoes, and white work shirt to and from the restaurant, so he could put away his shortcoat and take out his overcoat by feel, even though his locker was one that got some light from the hall. He did not use a lock. His keys to his building and his rooms never left his pocket.

"How come you gave him the checks?" Eddie Loo asked him.

"He is past helping," Bogart said.

"They saw it, you know," Eddie Loo said. "O'Meara. Chick."

Hero nodded, but he was already well outside the toilet by now, outside of talk and as good as gone into his silence along the sidewalk, into the stillness of sitting, of wiping clean, of waiting to return. He touched at the pocket that held his keys, and stepped past Bogart and Eddie Loo toward his locker.

"They watched the whole thing," Eddie Loo said. "From when he first started looking. They were waiting for it. That's why they gave him the kid."

Yes, he was gone. But home?

Was Hero gone to a kid and a green grass evening?

Or was he in a saloon not twenty blocks from here with his lousy son already dead. Dancing in a place that smelled as bad as this with a drunken tramp who called his good son a fairy for coming from college to make friends with his old man. He chose the tramp; he chose her and danced her and was glad, and never saw the boy leave.

To Eddie Loo, Hero said, "I didn't know he was looking."

"He didn't tell anybody," Eddie Loo said. "He is afraid now, so he just wanders around, looking."

"You're not helping, Man," Bogart said to Hero. "You make it worse for him. You drag it out. They are going to get rid of him. They give him to Andy to finish it off, and if you let it happen, he's gone. If he's on the floor, he makes trouble for everybody."

"And he costs money," Eddie Loo said.

"Every time I am next to him," Bogart said, "my customers have to listen to his people complain. You think that makes money for me? You think it makes money for you when you are next to him?"

"With the union," Eddie Loo said, "they can't fire him, but if he is bad enough, he will go when they tell him. If he thinks he can last, then they have to make it hard for him."

The two of them filed through the garbage in the hall. Bogart said, "So maybe he thinks he can last. Good. Let them squeeze him. He has it coming. He is a son of a bitch."

Hero turned to his locker, and heard their voices from the other side of the garbage, from the foot of the stairs up to the street. "Hello, Frenchman," Bogart said.

"Hello, Chinaman One," the Frenchman said. "Hello, Chinaman Two."

Eddie Loo's voice came then from what must have been halfway up the stairs. "You got any spare checks, Frenchman?"

"What is that to you? I know my checks, and they are none of your business. Chinaman. Where are your checks? You think I don't know more about table service than you will ever dream of? I have worked in real restaurants."

The iron street door swung shut, and the Frenchman's steps edged through the garbage. Hero looked deeply into his locker as though he imagined something else in there beside his over-coat.

"They would never have helped me," the Frenchman said behind Hero. "The fucking Chinamen."

Hero remained bowed into the darkness of his locker.

"That is why I do not tell anyone I am missing the checks. Maybe they tell Chick and O'Meara. Managers, they call them-selves. In a real restaurant they could not be dishwashers. What do I need from them? In a steakhouse."

The locker was eight inches across, and deep enough for the width of a hanger, angled. Hero took his overcoat out and held it over one arm as he unbuttoned the brassed button at the front of his white shortcoat and tried to shake his other arm out of its sleeve. It was such a light coat that it did not fall off easily. He shook that arm. He worked with his face close to his locker.

"They think I can't take care of my customers? In a place like this? The Chinese gangsters? I put my checks down. What business is that of theirs? I laugh at them. At all of them. I can serve the whole floor by myself, if I have to. And I do have to. They give me Andy now. Everybody sees that. So I am alone. I know what they are doing. I can still take care of my customers. That is the sort of waiter I am. I have customers everywhere who know me. That is who I take care of. That is my loyalty. Not to the Irish drunk at the desk. I am a true waiter, and they resent me."

Hero turned around because the Frenchman had gotten loud enough to sound ill.

There was a quivering from his jowls and the tops of his thick loose cheeks, and he did not look at Hero. He looked above Hero as though in confrontation with something blindly his own, to which he had had to explain himself many times before.

Hero stuffed his overcoat between his knees and with both hands pulled off his white waiter's coat.

"Hello," the Frenchman said. Now he saw Hero. In the, "Hello," was recognition, and abandonment to unhappiness. He nodded to Hero, trying it seemed to think what else to say.

Hero had his overcoat between his knees and held the white waiter's jacket in front of himself. Maybe the Frenchman would turn, and Hero could fold the coat gently over the Frenchman's shoulders and the Frenchman would go consoled out through the garbage and into the night in two layers of white coats.

"Over the bread?"

"Yes," Hero said.

"I cannot do it."

"You can," Hero said. "Sure you can." Sounding to himself insanely eager.

"I would quit if I had anywhere to go. My wife has died. I do not want to sit home. If she were alive she would not let me. If we were in France instead of here, she would have left me long ago. They were over the bread?"

"Between the charge slips," Hero said.

"I was never good enough. I have been in all of them. I have known all the maître d's. I was always wrong. Once I had a few nights at Lutece, but Soltner's wife I think did not like me. My wife knew it before I did. Now even the drunk Irishman knows it. And Bogart."

Hero looked at the set of brassed buttons holding closed the Frenchman's jacket. They were joined by a small brassed link. When you turned in your jacket, you kept your buttons to use with the clean jacket.

"What should I do?"

Hero shook his head in sympathy.

The Frenchman might have been about to cry. He actually expected an answer from Hero. He looked at Hero. Waited.

Hero waited too.

He waited for the Frenchman's failure to pass. The Frenchman's life. He closed his eyes and waited for the Frenchman to
die. But the Frenchman reached and touched Hero's bare hand,
and Hero backed against the door of his locker, and that banging rattle startled as if it were part of the Frenchman's fingers
upon him.

"Do your best," he said.

The Frenchman's mouth made a wry little grimace in his
soft face, and finally he did slide past Hero into the pit and to
his own locker where he put on his glasses and bent his face to
his lock. Hero hung up his white coat and closed his locker.

"An animal. They make me an animal. I cannot see to get out
my private clothes. Am I supposed to walk home like this? Am I
supposed to sleep on the floor in the wet? It is a sewer, and they
tell me now I am not good enough. I cannot have my clothes."

Hero went, and by standing out of the way of what brightness there was from the hall, could make out the numbers. He
waited for the Frenchman to tell him the combination, but
there was silence. "I can see," Hero said, and still the Frenchman was silent. "Your clothes would be too small for me," Hero
said.

"I keep my wallet in there."

"Then you better not leave any money in it."

"Twelve, eighteen, thirty-six."

The sound of voices came from out and down the hall, and
the Frenchman opened his door and busied himself with taking
off his bow tie and his jacket. Hero, going out, was stopped by
the Frenchman's call. "You." Hero looked back, and after having faced again the brightness of the hall garbage, he could not
distinguish a figure. "You are my only friend," the Frenchman
said.

Hero said, "Thank you." And though he could not see, Hero
faced a moment longer toward the Frenchman so that the
Frenchman might have that appearance of care.

Bruce and Henke came around the corner of the toilet's over-flow as Hero threaded through the garbage to the stairs.

"Hero my dearo," Bruce shouted, and waved largely enough to fill the hall. Henke smiled snidely, but Bruce's exuberance was happy. "We are free for another few hours from our fetters of food, our chains of protein, free from the great beef of life. Good-night, my Hero, enjoy. Who's in the pit to entertain us?"

Hero said, "Good night," and, "The Frenchman."

"You mean Giggles himself?" Bruce said, projecting his voice loudly toward the pit. Henke made a noise to go with his snide smile, and they advanced through the garbage. Hero, as he reached the iron street door, heard Bruce's voice shouting, "Clunk your magic twanger, Froggy."

The other schedule besides the weekly one was the daily. This was taped to the top of the maître d's desk each night before the service, and it told who worked which station, and who was a front man and who was back. It did not change too much from night to night. Bogart was the only young waiter who did not work the back. The others who didn't work the back were Hussein, Hero, the Mexican and the Frenchman, all of whom were old, though the Frenchman was not so old as Hero and Hussein, and the Mexican was not so old as the Frenchman.

But the next night the cooks told Hussein that Fat Tom had been in, and before service the Frenchman walked through the empty dining room with delicate feet, looking for signals. The other waiters showed nothing. The Frenchman looked at the daily schedule and went, as back men did, to choose a guéridon, to fold a tablecloth onto it. He penned his name across the top of the cloth.

When that was done, Fedy Llosa said, "That's right. You are a back man. My back man, and you are going to work tonight. You hear me, you lazy French fucker? You want any tip from me, you go fast."

For the first couple of parties, deuces, the Frenchman brought appetizers, and then went down and brought up the main courses. There was another deuce, a five, and a four, all at once.

Hero saw the Bolivian go to O'Meara to protest it was too much at once for the Frenchman. O'Meara could not hear.

Hero watched the appetizers come out more or less on time, watched the Bolivian running to cover the first deuces and the new drinks and wine and the new appetizers. The Frenchman was not out on the floor, and the Bolivian was clearing the appetizers at the same time he was resetting the early deuces. Chick brought a new deuce and O'Meara followed with another. The Bolivian could not leave the floor, and there was no evidence of the Frenchman anywhere. The deuce, the five, the four, none of them regulars, none parties for the house to worry about, sat waiting for main courses.

Hero found the Frenchman sitting on an extra chair, against the spare sink in the corner beneath the espresso pots. The kitchen was flooded with waiters and food and dishes, with the bustle of the dishwashers and the shouts between partners and the slippery navigation of all the guéridons loaded either with food or waste. In their rush, the other waiters slowed just enough to study the Frenchman with the curiosity given to gore on a fast highway. The Frenchman returned none of the looks, and Hero did not bother to speak to him.

In the lower kitchen, waiting to pick up on the line, were Castro, the Yugoslav, and Andy.

"Who's minding our *tienda?*" Castro said.

"The Frenchman sat down."

"He did what?" shouted the broiler man who ran the line at night. "Food fucking everywhere for him."

"I'll pick him up." Hero pulled the Frenchman's dupes, and the broiler man called them and immediately started feeding plates. Castro took off the side dishes, and Hero took the other plates as the broiler man put them up.

"Where is the motherfucker?" the broiler man shouted as he turned plate after plate. "I hear from him every fucking night when he is front man. One night in the back, and I got his fucking plates coming out my ass."

Hero stacked the plates and covers and laid a cloth and set a new tray on top. Castro pulled off the small vegetables and the two large fries. "Can you carry that?" Castro said.

Hero had not thought of it.

"On your stomach for up the stairs," Castro said. "Always. That is what I drink beer for."

"Where's your béarnaise?" the broiler man shouted.

The Yugoslav reached a monkey dish of béarnaise at the steam table, and Hero reached down the line to take it.

And Andy stepped inside of Hero to the trays.

Andy was going to take them. On his shoulder. "I got it," he said, affecting a deeper voice than was normal for him. He was not stable with a tray of any great weight. He squatted under these two doubled trays and said, "I'll be right back, Chef."

"I'm not any fucking chef, you asshole." Then the broiler man said, "Who's next?"

But the broiler man watched with Castro and the Yugoslav and Hero as Andy was led away by the stack of loaded trays he would never catch up to.

As soon as he was out of sight, around to the stairs, the noise of it came like an explosion of nothing else but heavy crockery and cement, cushioned only by sliding food and the soft bangs of the tin covers which rolled like hubcaps back into view. Andy came after them, holding the empty trays.

"Clean it up, Motherfucker," the broiler man said with an odd, calm satisfaction.

Hero went to the stairs, and when he passed Andy, Andy made a nervous smile. Almost a laugh.

Then as Hero was going up the stairs, hurrying to get back to his own station, as the broiler man was shouting at Andy,

"Don't fucking stand there. Clean it up," then the Frenchman came down the stairs slowly, innocent of Hero, innocent of his exploded food.

HAPPILY

Hero stood at his busing stand taking down folded napkins for a setup, and Chick led Molly from the desk. She had a reservation. She had asked for Hero, and Hero had kept the table for her. Once she was down the steps, she brushed Chick away and waved happily and came on alone to her corner. Came to Hero. It was she and Hero that were friends. She had a bright quick wave and almost a skip to her walk. She might have been a girl. Hero did not think to wave until she was too close for a wave not to seem silly. But he said, "Hi," and he forgot to take her to her table because she was so plainly coming to see him. He stood beside his busing stand with its pile of folded linen napkins and its stack of ready ashtrays and butter plates and its scatter of stains. What to say?

"I'm glad you came," he said, not really worried about what to say.

"I'm glad I came too," she said, standing right before him, with eyes as curious and gay as open water on a summer morning. What a nice size she was. "But we can't keep meeting like this," she said. "I'm too old to stand for long anymore, especially if I have to dodge the carts. And between my neck and my digestion, I don't do well sitting and looking up at you to talk while I eat alone and duel with your colleague Castro.

I've become a one task at a time girl, and even that I have to keep on a single level of eye contact."

Something was funny and Hero began a chuckle. He could see that she was pleased with his smile. And with his laugh too. Something was lewd, and she must have seen that in his laugh.

"Then I'll take my shoes off," he said, and out of Molly's amusement came a bark of real laughter. She stood as if she expected him to say more and them to laugh more, and he had a sense, nearly tangible, of himself with a drink and with the flush of things in his face.

Which gave directly to her own mention of eating and of Castro. Hero was a waiter, and he felt for his keys. He turned from her and started so suddenly for her table, to pull it out and seat her, that he nearly collided with Robert pushing a guéridon through.

"Watch the fuck out," Robert hissed. "Or we send you back to geriatrics."

Hero went again at the table and pulled it out and said, "Here you are, Madam."

As she slid with some difficulty behind the table, she said quietly, "Molly."

"Molly," he said.

This was Tuesday, and Andy had the Frenchman's night, in front, and he also had the Yugoslav who was both a wonderful back man and silent. Chick and O'Meara fed Andy tables on a perfect break, so that the Yugoslav could have done the whole night alone, and almost did. Andy handed out menus. Chick and O'Meara gave Andy perfect parties, one after another. Andy raked in money. Andy was delighted. Andy flirted with his tables, was young and coy and shy. Then he stepped away to stand with other waiters, pretending to be embarrassed at all the money he was making. He stepped over to stand by Hero, but Hero was busy and moved off. Andy stopped over by the old Iranian's stand, to discuss some of a waiter's business, but

Hussein was also busy. Even Henke was too busy for Andy. Andy patrolled among his tables with the humility of great importance and great wealth, and Hero watched him arch his eyebrows and flick his head in the way of a greeting across the room to the two Chinese waiters in their high corner. Bogart, who saw everything, did not see Andy. Eddie Loo, who was crouched at his guéridon bringing sauces and spoons, without the loss of a motion gave Andy the finger. Bruce came past Andy, pushing a guéridon. Bruce was so large and gangling that the guéridon came little higher than his knees, and with his happy, playful face he appeared an overgrown child pushing a toy. When he had passed Andy, he slapped a large hand on Andy's shoulder and laughed, and by the time Andy had manufactured a graceful greeting, Bruce had taken his laugh on along with his guéridon to his station.

Molly this time had come in earlier than other times, and she and Hero, after their first conversation, could for a while only speak in passing.

"Why do you watch that boy?" she asked.

Hero shrugged and shook his head.

When he came to persuade a dessert, after Castro had gotten her plate and taken her coffee order, Molly said, "I don't think I like that boy. I can spot the awful ones, because I've raised several."

"I don't like him."

"I try not to like mine, but I don't really have the stomach for it."

"I hate him," Hero said, and found himself suddenly so choked with hatred that he could barely finish speaking. "I hate him, and I'm not ashamed."

He went away without an order for her dessert. He stood at the busing stand and pressed his fists down onto the linen. In Andy's station, the Yugoslav was cracking lobsters for a prime four, and Andy was gone. Hero went to look in the kitchen, and by the long dishwashers' counter, Andy was drinking from a beer bottle. You could get fired for drinking in the middle of the service in the middle of the kitchen from the bottle. Andy held the bottle to the Polack. The Polack pushed his loaded guéridon past and out; Hero went back to the floor himself. Robert had come to help the Yugoslav get the lobsters out. It was not such a busy night, and now it was getting late. Robert had time and the Yugoslav had time.

Hero got the dessert cart and rolled it back and opened it so that the desserts gave out at Molly as if from a glass casket.

"I'm sorry," he said to the display of wrinkling fruits and careless pastries.

"You were upset."

"I'm a waiter."

"I'm in New York because my father is ill. Dying, actually. He always liked a steakhouse in Brooklyn, and I don't want to have to go to Brooklyn. I don't even really like a steakhouse. I want to be with somebody who is my friend from somewhere other than the hospital. I want to hear why you don't like that boy, though I don't want to pry. And I want you to take your desserts away, unless Castro says I have to have one." To Castro who had come up behind Hero, she said, "Do I have to have something?"

Castro stepped in past the glass dessert casket and whispered loudly, "We must try and sell these to your neighbors, and if you do not buy, you are not helping. Also, you hold down the check average. I told the Haitian to save me a good melon. I will bring it for you, and if you can't eat it, then I will have it."

"It's too cold out for melon."

"I like it with a little salt. I will bring it."

Castro went away to the kitchen, and Molly was pleased. Hero asked, "How do you know his name?"

"I asked the fashion plate at the front. Chick."

"Chick?"

"He introduced himself. But now you answer a question. Tell me something about yourself. Anything. If you won't tell me about the boy, tell me how you came here. I'll tell you how I did. I've told you, really."

"You came in the front door, Molly, and I came in the back."

"That's not very fair, when I came in, whatever door it was, just to see you."

There were two other tables waiting to look at the desserts, and Hero said, "I shouldn't have told you I hated that boy."

"Of course you should have. I'm sorry. I certainly don't need to know how you got here."

"He can't do the work, so the managers are letting him have good parties and make money for a couple of days before they throw him out. And he doesn't get it. That's their joke. In fact he thinks he's a big shot all of a sudden, which is more of a laugh than they'd hoped for."

Hero turned and pulled the desserts away for the other tables.

"Thank you," Molly said after him, and Castro came from the kitchen with her melon.

ANDY BABY

"Andy Baby."

"Andy, Baby. How are you doing?"

"Yo. Andy. How's a man?"

It was Friday, and Hero had not worked Wednesday and Thursday, but Andy had, and it all must have been fine, because Andy came through the dining room as if he were an old hand. Shy still, pushing up his glasses and aw-shucksing, but he now was one of the boys, and a front man, and had made a bill for the past several nights. He had not however yet seen this evening's daily schedule. Nor had he seen the book, though he would not think to look at the book anyhow. He had not heard the cooks downstairs say that Fat Tom had been in during the afternoon.

The Yugoslav was off. The daily schedule had the Bolivian as Andy's back man. And there were already a hundred and eighty on the book, enough that Bogart and Eddie Loo were in to help.

O'Meara and Chick had made it smooth for Andy on the nights when the restaurant's regulars came in, to keep the regulars happy. Tonight, O'Meara and Chick would feed Andy to the Friday night assholes, and to Fedy Llosa. Everyone but Fedy watched Andy check the daily schedule. The Bolivian was late coming in.

Castro yelled across stations to the Polack wiping his knives, "Hundred and eighty already, Martina. What do you think?"

"There's no more. Nobody is in town. Two hundred twenty. I will make a bill and you will make sixty. Like always."

"You hear the Polack, Andy? He says two-twenty. How crazy is Martina, Andy?"

Andy didn't know what they were talking about.

"People, Andy. And dogs and cats and *muertos*. On the book. They are all coming tonight, Andy Baby. I say two hundred and eighty."

"Leave the kid alone," Robert said. "You'll upset him. We won't do two-fifty. But as usual the rest of us will have to make up for you getting stuck, Castro."

"Robert," Bruce called from his far front corner. "Don't you get fussy so early in the evening. Andy can take care of himself perfectly well without your help. Andy can handle it if we do four hundred, can't you Andy. Just don't let Robert try to fluster you."

"I'm not trying to fluster him, you faggot."

"Stop it, Robert. I won't stand for you becoming cranky before I've finished my sidework."

"Two seventy-five," Eddie Loo said.

"Andy and I think it is going to be two-eighty," Castro said.

"We will do over three hundred," Bogart said, managing to say it quietly and be heard throughout the dining room. "There are two conventions."

"Who are the conventions?" the Polack called.

"Read the fucking papers, Martina," Bogart said.

"I think it is three hundred also."

"So do I," Andy said.

"Three hundred, Andy?" Castro said. "You and Señor Fedy Llosa will be very very busy if it is three hundred."

"Leave the little fucker alone, Castro. He couldn't be any slower than you."

"Robert. Don't you dare speak to my friend Castro like that."

"And you," Robert said, "don't deserve to work at an automat."

"Do you hear how Robert's behaving?"

"And don't run to Princess Henke once you've started something."

"I don't mind three hundred," Andy said.

"You better hope I'm wrong by a hundred," Bogart said quietly.

"I like it when it's busy," Andy said.

"That's a boy," Robert said.

"Robert," Henke called. "Don't touch that boy."

"Look," Castro said. "*Buenas tardes*, Señor Llosa. *Trabajas con el* Andy."

As the Bolivian walked through the dining room from the kitchen, he watched at Castro, and then at Bogart.

"*La verdad*," Castro said. "*Estas abajo don* Andy. And tonight it is so busy that Bogart and Eddie Loo come to visit. Look, you see your friend Chick?"

Chick was at the far side of the desk on the phone, taking reservation after reservation.

"Look at the book, Bolivian," the Polack said.

Fedy Llosa looked at the schedule, and the book, and came down the three steps to the floor. "Fuck you, Martina," he said, and headed at his station where Andy waited with his hands hanging from his narrow wrists. Bruce stepped out and swung a long arm around the Bolivian's shoulders.

"Fedy," Bruce said. "We are so happy to see you. I want you to know . . . "

The Bolivian threw off Bruce's arm. "Fuck you in the ass, Frankenstein."

Chick, as he held the phone and wrote into the book, watched the action on the floor.

From his own station, Hero watched.

Andy pushed up his glasses with a forefinger and then held that hand back down in front of himself again, and smiled at Fedy Llosa who'd reached him and who stared at him.

Andy made a smile. He held out his hand now as though to shake. He was a front man. A bill-a-night man. He said, "I guess it's you and I tonight, Fedy."

The Bolivian stared, rocking his upper body which was so disproportionately larger than his short legs.

Hero watched, and up out of the bottom of his stomach, he manufactured a massing of hatred too violent for language. And he gave that into unspeakable hope for the surface of the Bolivian to burst, for the Bolivian to damage Andy.

Andy brought back his unshaken hand and dropped both hands down to his sides, but could not bring his shoulders and his neck erect. In the periphery around him were the other waiters' grins. "We're doing three hundred," Andy said. "We'll have to move."

For one teetering moment, it seemed about to happen. Then it was past.

Fedy Llosa laughed. "You hear that?" he said. "Eat your heart out, Frankenstein. Andy wants me tonight. Three hundred times." Fedy jumped around behind Andy and made as if to hump him and grinned now at Bogart and Eddie Loo, though they did not laugh. "That's right, Andy Baby. You and me tonight. In and out, in and out." The rest laughed though, as the Bolivian worked his pelvis at the back of Andy's thighs. "Three hundred tonight, Andy Baby." Andy laughed with them. He was a front man and a bill-a-night man, a man who'd already forgotten burying the Frenchman.

The people were from out-of-town, and dogs, and so many that the service was thrown at them as the the kitchen backed up. But Chick and O'Meara gave Andy only a couple of early parties of sitters, and then an easy staggered break. Andy was running where anyone else would have been walking. But he was afloat, because Chick and O'Meara paced him. Hero figured what was happening, and even so resented Chick and O'Meara putting it off. One of Andy's tables was an extender which could take ten, but on that they had put an early four, and when the four was gone, they had had Andy set it for another four, busy as the restaurant was. Hero himself was running, and Castro was stuck, but Hero kept an eye on Andy's station, on Fedy Llosa snatching the dupes from Andy and directing Andy and swearing at Andy, though they were still afloat. Andy was not nearly panicked. Andy thought he was handling a three hundred night.

Molly was at the desk, and after Chick brought her down the stairs she made to come on by herself, through the forest of extra chairs and the rush of guéridons and the loud heat of the full room. She looked tired and confused, and she searched for Hero. She should have been able to see him. Most of the crowd were sitting after all. Hero had had to force a deuce, but he'd opened up her table for her. She was lost. She stopped. Why couldn't she just let Chick bring her? She was too small and she was baffled by the clamor. She could not see Hero, though she knew perfectly well where his station was. Hero tore dupes for Castro, and wondered if she could hold there until he'd got the drink order on the five. She looked as if she might weep, and she was blocking traffic for the waiters. That would be Hero's fault of course. He went to get her, and she did not even see him until he was to her, and then her face was such ridiculous relief that Hero could not wrench up a smile.

Only then did he see how thoroughly Chick and O'Meara had set it up. One of Andy's fours had to leave at a specific time and was getting up now directly from main courses. One of his deuces was empty. Andy was standing back on his heels as if he had made it through the big night. Chick was signaling to Andy, and at first Andy did not even notice.

Molly was speaking to Hero, but Hero grinned above and beyond her to the desk. Chick and O'Meara had collected a horde of people behind them, and Chick was holding his hands out at Andy with nine fingers showing. Flashing, nine, to Andy, and then pointing at the big extension table which Andy had set for four. Chick signaled for six more on the table where the four had just gotten up from main courses.

Then Chick came leading a couple to Andy's open deuce. Andy stood, wondering.

"May we go to the table, Hero," Molly said.

Chick had a few steps on the couple, and in the crowd could say to Andy, almost at the level of regular speech, "Move your ass, Shithead. You got seventeen sitting. The nine and the six are at the desk. Give me tables. Now, Asshole. Now." Chick smiled the deuce into their seats and as he came back said again to the immobile Andy, "Tables, Shithead," in a voice like a baseball bat to the face. Hero thrilled to that voice, and to Andy suddenly hearing and realizing. Panicking.

"Please, Hero. I don't like to have to stand here."

Hero clenched his jaw. He led her to the corner and seated her. He had the five. He had Castro bringing four chickens to bone for four cheapskates.

"I'm sorry Molly. It's busy." Hero gave her a menu. He took the drinks on the five, and as he went at the bar he watched Fedy Llosa push Andy to the stand for silver and linen as he pulled the extenders. Andy had the face of a cow chased by boys with stones, and Chick brought the nine even as the Bolivian sprawled across the table throwing silver and napkins randomly. Chick smiled and turned back for the six, and the Bolivian turned and dove to set that six, and Andy could think of nothing to do but pull out chairs for the children on the nine, until the Bolivian ripped at his arm and drove him at the stand again for more linen and more silver. The deuce waited unattended. Another four needed to be cleared. Another deuce waited for dessert. Andy bumped into chairs getting to the stand. Chick came with the six. Chick was graceful and delighted. O'Meara at the desk took a moment to watch it all. Hero thrilled to it. Hero urged the violence filling the Bolivian.

Hero set the drinks and menus for the five. Castro came with the guéridon and he and Hero tore and split the chickens. Hero totaled two deuces and went to Molly.

She had not decided. She didn't speak. She was as lost as Andy. Hero left her with the menu.

The Bolivian came again at Andy, and pushed both hands hard into his back. In nearly a shout he said, "What the fuck's the matter with you? Move, motherfucking faggot. Move." Hero's stomach churned for willing the violence. Not later, not hidden in the basement. Right here, now.

And it came. Fedy shoved Andy so hard that Andy stumbled and fell to the floor, and Fedy stood over him in a madness, readying to kick at him, as Hero grabbed menus from his own stand and took more menus from the Polack as he passed.

In two more steps Hero was beside the Bolivian as Andy tried to stand. Hero grabbed Andy and pulled him up and spun him around by his jacket.

"Give me your fucking checks," Hero shouted into Andy's waffled face. Andy did nothing, and Hero grabbed inside the jacket for the checks and punched the menus into Andy's chest so hard that Andy lurched back against the post behind his stand.

"Give them, Asshole. Hand them out," and Hero smacked with his fist into Andy's shoulder. Andy began at least to do that, to pass the menus, and Hero went to the deuce with two more menus and smiled and bowed for them and recommended for them as if there were time now for all the patience in the world. He got a drink order. He handed a check so the Bolivian could get drinks on the six.

He turned back to the nine, five of them kids, and called out as Andy put down the last of the menus, "Red meat tonight. Please. Have the strip and the prime rib. The small strip if the ladies insist. No Sir, it's too busy for any of that. And too busy for me to be funny, if I ever were funny. Now what would you like to drink? Yes. Good. Scotch. No, Madam, the bartender won't make fancy drinks when I'm in a hurry. Have a beer. Good. Tab? You kids all sissies? Okay. Okay. Got it. When I get back you can tell me how you like your meat. It all comes medium rare. Andy, take care of the going tables for Christ sake. Nobody talk to Andy, or you'll distract him. Move it, Andy. The going tables, nothing else."

He brought drinks and wrote dupes on the deuce and the nine. He took the six after the Bolivian got their drinks. He took the order on his own five. He ran cards on the four and the deuce. He took Eddie Loo's guéridon for the apps on the nine and that deuce, then the five. Castro cleared and reset the deuce and the four. Hero ran at Andy, who simply stood.

"You got these?" he shouted. "You got these?" Hero took the checks on the running tables and totaled and laid them down. He went to the six and said to the guy with the stomach and the wallet, "May I bring two bottles of a good twenty dollar cabernet here?"

"If you're buying," the fat guy said, and got laughs from his pals.

"If I were buying for women as handsome as these, I would bring two of the sixty dollar bottles."

"Great," the fat guy said. The others laughed.

"I can't afford it," Hero said. He was sorry. He leaned and confessed that to the very important fat guy. "I wish that I could."

"Well I can afford it," the fat guy said. "Bring two of the sixty."

"This isn't going to cut into my tip, is it?"

And the fat guy said, "Who the fuck is this character?" as if all the laughter were his own cleverness.

"I owe you a cognac," Hero said, which certified that it had been in fact the fat guy's cleverness, and Hero grabbed Andy.

"Two bottles of the Mondavi Reserve. Two. The Reserve. Go."

Hero and Fedy Llosa served main courses, and Eddie Loo brought the back guéridon with the rest of the plates.

Hero main-coursed the five and had only one new deuce, and the night was stringing out suddenly and they were clear and his fury was gone and he was wet with sweat and he smiled at the empty post above his stand where all the napkins had been stacked at the start of the service. Smiled with the release of coming out the other side of frenzied effort. High from that release.

He had left Molly. Sitting there in the corner with her menu.

He stepped to Castro. "Did you take Molly?"

"No, Man. I thought you want to do your girl friend. I said Hello, but she didn't ask nothing from me."

He went to her corner. "I'm sorry, Molly." He was sorry, but he was exultant too. He had left her all this time. Really, it was funny. "What'll ya have?" he said, and grinned and brought out her check and posed as a caricature of a waiter at pad.

"That's all right," she said. Hero knew it was all right. She sat back as if she was exhausted from sitting. She still didn't know what she wanted.

"What's an hour when you can be in a great place like this?" he said and laughed, full of the confidence of his success.

"What were you doing?"

"Running," he said, so satisfied that he was prepared to brag. He had carried the two stations, fifty covers.

"You were helping the boy."

"What?"

"That boy you said you hated. You were kind to him, weren't you." It seemed to wear her out just to say that much.

"I forgot you, Molly. I'm sorry. If you're angry, be angry. Tell me what you want to eat. I'll rush it. I'll even buy it."

"You said you hated him, and then you went to him when he was lost." She was so worn out she looked like she should be cleared with the old linen.

Hero overflowed with energy and impatience. "You want a drink, Molly? Let me buy a drink. I'm sorry I forgot you."

"I don't want a drink, Hero. I'm sorry." Barely even a noise to her voice.

"Well, what the hell do you want, Molly? For Christ sake. If you don't want food and you don't want a drink, why don't you go back to your fucking hospital and die with your father." And now it was as if Hero were back in the middle of the effort and frenzy. He was sweating again and his breath had begun to come furiously again. Drunk.

Molly slid and stood from the table, and as she did she fished in her small bag and brought out a couple of twenty dollar bills and dropped them beside her menu.

Hero clenched his hands to fists, and his jaws as tight as his fists, and Molly floated away.

TO OUR PICNIC

Floated away.

The five were ready for dessert. The late deuce was on track. The other deuce open. The four almost to a check. The other four a no-show on the last turn; Chick probably gave them away when Hero was bailing out Andy. And Molly's deuce, empty.

The five, running out of money, wanted a check instead of dessert. Hero totaled them and closed out the four. The night was done. Hero felt as if he too might be floating, and multiplied the eight-and-a-quarter in his head and dropped both checks to their tables.

Castro came out of the kitchen with his empty guéridon, ready for a dessert order, and when he saw the checks down on the five and the four he grinned. The restaurant had been a kennel all night; nobody was making money except Bogart, and if Castro could get out early with bus fare, Castro was happy. Castro looked at Molly's table. He walked over and picked up the two twenties she'd left there.

Hero picked up cards on the five and the four and went to the kitchen to run those. But when he came back and put down the slips, Castro still held the two twenties, and he looked at Hero from there beside Molly's table.

"Where is our beauty?"

Hero picked up the menu she'd left.

"She was angry? I let her down?"

"No," Hero said.

"You had a fight."

Hero shrugged.

"That's good. A fight is good. But what is this?" Castro held out the money. "When she was a stranger you gave her back forty of our dollars. Now that she comes a couple of times and is our friend, now you keep the money when she hasn't made the napkin dirty. What's the matter with you tonight? You're so busy for this *maricón* Andy . . . "

"You keep it," Hero said, and went to Andy's station.

"This is dirty money," Castro said after him. "You get arrested for spending money like this."

Andy was functional again. Fedy Llosa was clearing the messes. The deuce was paying. The fat big shot on the six called to Hero. "Hey, Dad. Where you been?"

Hero smiled and said, "That's right. I owe you a cheap brandy."

Out of the laughter of the rest of the table the fat guy squealed, "Cognac, George. Cognac."

Hero went on their laughter to the bar, and Castro, drinking from the cart, watched him. Fedy Llosa stopped him on the way back. "What the fuck is that?" the Bolivian said.

"I promised him a drink when it was busy at the start," Hero said, and went by, and put the brandy down to the fat guy without hearing any more of that table's voices.

Castro still watched him, while hitting on the fake Irish whiskey off the cart.

Hero turned his back on Castro.

He could go to the party of nine, with all its kids. They would need something. One of the kids in fact was watching him now. She was a child, eleven, sixteen, fourteen. How could Hero know an age? She was alive and beginning.

As if it was as simple as rain off a new leaf, she looked like she could be proud of anyone.

Hero stood where he was. He did not want to turn again at Castro, and now he wished that he did not have to be seen by this girl either.

She looked at Hero, studied him. And she giggled.

No. Not sobs or tears. But his face clenched against them. And with his wrong hand patting for comfort at the wrong pants pocket and finding no keys, Hero must have been funny to look at.

He straightened himself and got moving. He walked around the table to behind her chair and leaned to the side of her blond head, the hair of which had been particularly curled at some point but was now just frizzy at the edges. She smelled like a baby, and that smell — though what had Hero ever had to do with babies? — swam with the presumption of forgiveness.

He said, "How was your pheasant, My Dear? Properly boned? Not too dry?"

She blushed. Her two girl friends looked prepared to be alarmed. But this child of Hero's, once she had exercised her blush, looked again at Hero and giggled again. The other two girls, fast as children's dams gone to a busy stream, burst with giggles also. Hero was funny for all of them to look at.

He arched his eyebrows. "The pheasant was not right?" He looked around the table. There were two boys, the girls' age, and they were sure Hero was a jerk. They were in sport coats and club ties. The parents were too proper to have been caught in this place unless it were to amuse the kids. That was it; it was the first of Christmas vacation, and the parents were delighted to have Hero distract these barely teenagers home from boarding school.

So Hero did that; he distracted. He said to the boys, "Would you gentlemen mind if I bought these young women after-dinner drinks?"

"Yes, yes." A drink in a mid-town steakhouse. The girls wanted — and they knew what they wanted — brandy alexanders, whiskey sours, tequila sunrises.

"Be quiet," Hero said to them. "I know what you want." To the adult end of the table, he said, "Cognac? My treat."

Hero went to Castro and handed him the check for the last deuce to total. He took the two twenties that Castro still held. Castro had had any number more hits off the cart, and maybe he could add the deuce, maybe not. He stared at Hero. Hero went to the bar for five half-shots of Gran Marnier for the kids, in shot glasses for the boys and in ponies for the girls, and then four cognacs for the adults. He put out the twenties to the barman.

"You kidding me, Hero? These are comps. Right? I decide what drinks to comp around here. Pick up your money."

"Keep it for Yankee tickets in the spring."

"Here are your drinks, Hero. Put your bills in your pocket before I nail them to your head."

Hero picked up the twenties and said, "You're a kind man."

"What the fuck is that supposed to mean?" the barman said. "Around here."

Floated away.

Past the toilet and along the shuddering emptiness of the late subway to a door of his own that he could unlock and lock behind himself, to the safety of a varnished bureau and three windows, and then back the next night past the puddling reek of the toilet again to begin again.

And the next night, Saturday night, Fat Tom had already been in and gone, and on the evening's schedule of stations and positions Hero was listed to work as back man for Andy.

O'Meara called him over to the desk to be sure he saw. "We thought since you wanted to help Andy so much, you might as well eat the whole pig."

In the kitchen, Hero got a guéridon, laid fresh linen on the shelves and on its top, collected spare serving silver for it, and the spare shelling crackers and cocktail forks for lobsters, a handful of lemon halves and some extra monkey dishes. He collected ashtrays for the station. He folded napkins. Andy arrived, and Hero did not speak to him except to tell him to bring up the breads.

Across the cloth on top of his guéridon, Hero wrote his name. That was the practice. Each back man had his own guéridon for each night, and no one else was to use it for that night. All the food and all the cleared dishes theoretically had to be moved on the guéridons, so if people used each other's guéridons indiscriminately, somebody could get stuck without when he needed one. A back man's guéridon was personal property for the night, and each back man wrote his claim across the top of its covering linen. "Hero."

In the time before the service, after the sidework and the staff dinner, Hero shoved his guéridon among the other guéridons there in the kitchen, and sat across from them on a glassrack alone against his wall. He knew all there was to do. He understood the downstairs of the kitchen. He leaned over and he pressed the heels of his hands into the tops of his thighs; he massaged them, and he recollected that on the stairs Castro carried his trays out from his stomach. Hero rocked slowly backwards and forwards on his glass-rack, with his hands pressing into his thighs. If he was frightened, it was of trying to go fast down the stairs. If he tired and gave out coming up the stairs, perhaps he would be too tired to care, but he did not like to think about folding his ankle and pitching headlong down.

He rocked against his wall, bumped against his wall. And each time his back hit against the painted brick, it forced a word, a sylable, a sound, in a rhythm of unwanted verse: if you don't *want* — food and you *don't* — want a drink *why* — don't you go *back* — to your fucking *hos* — pital and *die* — with your father *if* — you don't want *food* — and you don't *want* — a drink why *don't* — you go back *to* — your fucking hos*pital* — and die with your *father*.

Then Andy came and stood before him. Andy with his hands hanging, with his head protruding, his glasses soiled. "You left last night before I could thank you for helping me out when it got so busy. I guess I got sort of stuck. So it's nice that we're working together tonight."

Hero closed his eyes.

And the boy went on in his nasal earnest falseness. "I mean I know I got stuck. But I think I can do better. I think. . . ."

Even with his eyes closed, Hero could see the boy's bitten knuckles. See all his posture of submissive cunning, from the knob at the back of his bent neck to the fidgeting shoes with their queerly worn heels. He was a boy outside whatever was normal, and then not just a crook but a man who would kill himself with drugs before anyone even knew what drugs were. One moment he was a black worm boring out from his mother, out of Alice and through their family, into the world to shame them all. The next moment his blackness had swollen and turned on them.

Fury surged in Hero because he knew every inch of that boy, and could not remember so much as one feature of his good boy. Alive, somewhere. Could not pretend to imagine him. It was all he could do to try and remember the girl on Andy's table of nine.

He opened his eyes. Andy.

Andy was tall and thin, and stood straight enough. Andy's hands did not hang before him and his knuckles were not bitten. His head did not reach forward dishonestly. This was the same boy who had finished the Frenchman and laughed, the same boy who now would finish Hero. But he was simply nineteen or twenty. He had a sound face and clear eyes, clean eyeglasses; he just didn't know how to work in a restaurant.

Even now, Andy looked at Hero, expecting some kind of direction.

"It's all right," Hero said, and Andy nodded as if that were the direction. Hero said, "Go sit down," and Andy nodded and stood there in front of Hero.

"So. Hero."

Fedy Llosa's voice came with the loud, flatted resonance which seemed part of his great jaw. It echoed with the careless precision of the daily schedule, and Hero paid no attention.

It was more important for Hero to know in his legs that if he could get the trays up the stairs, he would only have to put them on his guéridon and roll them out.

"Heero," Bruce said in a happy, rolling tease.

"Don't instigate," Robert said. "He's the only quiet one."

"So Hero," the Bolivian said, still louder.

Hero looked down at the damp red cement between his shoes, and pressed the heels of his hands into his thighs. There was a disconnected curiosity which peeked at the tunneling steepness of concrete steps, and listened for shattering crockery and slopped food and the bounce of tin plate covers. Hero rocked on his glass-rack against his wall, and the curiosity was a lure, a warning buoy in fog and the promise of falling a last time.

"So Hero. Here is a guéridon with your name on it. Does that mean you are a nigger tonight like the rest of us? Are you going to go up and down, up and down?"

As if he were a stranger to it, Hero made himself reach out for his litany, for the parts of his service. He did that, and he touched the bump his keys made beneath the black khaki of his pants.

"Leave him alone," Robert said. "He's not like you."

"He is like," Fedy called, "you, Robert."

"Robert," Bruce said. "For goodness sake don't egg him on. I won't have you involved in teasing, and neither will Henke."

"He is like you," Fedy Llosa called. "A faggot." The voice ran louder and higher, but still insistently surrounded its broad emptiness. "See what it says on Hero's guéridon? It says, Hero and Andy."

In fact, this part of his litany was strange. A back man. He paced himself through the physical motion of lifting the trays. He sat on his glass-rack against his wall, and he felt the weight of the trays and lifted, and took the distance from the end of the line to the stairs, and then up the stairs. One step. One step.

He sensed Andy looking over to try and see what the Bolivian was writing on the guéridon. He heard Andy trying to laugh with the rest of them. He said to Andy, "Don't laugh. Go out on the floor."

Hero looked at the red cement between his black, thick-soled shoes. The weight of the trays. He worked the heels of his hands against his thighs, but he felt the weight in his arms, holding the trays in front of himself, and taking the steps of the stairs, blind, his feet lost beneath the balancing plates and covers. One step up. One step up.

"I knew it last night when he couldn't stay away from Andy. Right Andy?"

Hero watched Andy's feet go away for the other end and the door out to the dining room.

"Look, Hero. Andy is shy. Andy won't tell us what you did to him while you were helping him. And Robert is jealous. Robert wants it, Hero."

"Hero," Bruce said. "Is this true? What you've written on the top of your guéridon?"

"If you drive this thing out on the floor," Henke said, "they're going to rip off your clothes, Hero."

"No, Hero," Bruce said. "You?"

"That's right," the Bolivian shouted. "He sucks Andy's cock. Every day for an hour."

"Well," Bruce said. "You shouldn't advertise it. Not these days."

"Hero likes to advertise," Fedy Llosa shouted. "And tonight he is going to help Chick. Aren't you, Hero? Hero is very helpful."

Bruce got up and brought a glass-rack over beside Hero, and sat next to Hero. He said, "I mean, do you know where Andy has been?"

"Hero only wants to suck cock," Fedy shouted. "He doesn't care where it's been."

Hero stood up to go, and stepped around Bruce, and felt the Bolivian's quick steps behind.

Before he could get there, before Fedy could reach and grab him from behind, Hero turned to face him.

"Listen," Castro said. "Hero has a girl friend. Hero is straight. He stole my beauty."

"Shut up, Castro," Fedy said. He stood immediately in front of Hero but did not look into Hero's face. He smiled at the other waiters. "Andy is Hero's girl friend. Hero and Andy."

"And I for one think it is as sweet as can be, Hero," Bruce said, balancing his own glass-rack back and forth in Hero's usual place, smiling up at Hero.

"You two are the *maricones*," Castro said. "Hero is a man."

Fedy Llosa ignored Castro, and ignored Hero standing in front of him. Into the waiters the Bolivian said, "But now he wants to have Chick for a girl friend too, so he has to ask Robert where Chick's cock has been. Isn't that right, Hero?"

He said that at the waiters, but then for an instant, he glanced with his great grin directly at Hero.

In that instant, Hero pushed at him with both hands. Hero leaned and pushed into the Bolivian's chest, and pushed hard enough to send the Bolivian backwards into the guéridons and the other waiters. The guéridons smacked, and rolled banging back against the extra sinks under the espresso pots. Fedy Llosa sprawled to his elbows on the guéridon he'd hit and on the seat of an empty chair. The other waiters jammed their own chairs back out of the way and fended off the loose guéridons.

Hero kicked at Bruce and caught, with his kick, Bruce's glass-rack as it tipped away from the wall. So that Bruce sat directly to the floor with his long arms caught up around his knees.

"God damn it," Hero shouted at Bruce, but Bruce only sat, with his happy grin.

Hero faced the Bolivian, who had stood up from the guéridons. Hero stood with his feet apart and with his arms out from his sides, with his hands in fists. "Come on," he said. "Come on, God damn you."

"You deserved it, Man," Castro said to Fedy. "Now leave him alone."

Fedy smiled quickly at Hero, and then around at the other waiters. "Calm down, Hero," he said, as much to the other waiters as to Hero.

"I mean it, God damn you," Hero said, and took a step at him.

"*Mira*," the Bolivian said. "*El viejo maricón furioso.*" He laughed to the other waiters, who did not now laugh. Castro stood up and rubbed his stomach. Eddie Loo was blind to any of it. Bogart was off. The Yugoslav watched. The Polack stood and said, "No fights."

The Bolivian smiled only to Hero now. "You hear *el Polacko*, Hero? No fights. The union says we get fired for fights."

"I don't care."

"Calm down, Hero," Fedy Llosa said, smiling and holding his hands out in front of himself as if to help calm, and also to make fun of the calming.

"You don't get it." Hero took another step at him. "I won't have it any more. Ever."

"Okay, Hero. You get out on the floor now. They want you on the floor."

"You understand?" Hero stood now face to face with him again. "You understand what I mean? No more."

"Okay, Hero. Careful or they think we are fighting."

"You understand? Or not?" Hero shouted this into his face.

"I understand, Hero," he said, and grinned around at the other waiters who only watched.

"It's not funny," Hero said, and stepped against him. And Fedy Llosa leaned back once more onto the guéridon he had fallen against.

He leaned back onto an elbow and grinned around himself, and then looked once seriously at Hero with his eyes half closed and with his face flat and his massive chin nearly to his chest. "I understand, Hero," he said.

Then he grinned again, as Chick came in from the dining room.

"Chick," Bruce shouted from his place on the floor. "You've come to our picnic. Sit down. We're having pears and lady fingers and . . . "

"Get the fuck up off the floor for Christ sake. Listen, you assholes. The book is loading up again. We're going to be busy as hell again. Hero, you get a reprieve. I'm putting you in front, with Castro. But from now on mind your own fucking business. You Andy, you're a back man, for the rest of your life. Work with the Polack tonight. Henke gets Llosa."

THANK CHRIST

Not often, and not in every restaurant, but sometimes, there was the moment before a fight when you made a noise or you didn't. Hero never made a noise; he kept quiet and went on to another restaurant. Yet here he had in fact made a noise. And maybe he would be hurt for it, maybe the Bolivian would still try to get him.

But it was having made the noise at all that was fearful.

Having taken Andy's station and having tried to help the Frenchman, those things, too, were fearful.

The touch of his keys, the half-height icebox that held his ice cream in its freezer, his canned soups on the two burner kitchenette, the television off — even in the middle of all this, Hero was afraid. His emptiness was broken, and the tin mirror on his medicine cabinet tried not to show its astonished regret.

But, "This Andy," Hussein said, "this Andy was supposed to disappear on Friday and Saturday. This motherfucking Andy should be on the street by now."

It was the next night, Sunday, and the old Iranian was looking at the new week's schedule on the wall across from the bread. Hero pushed, harder and more quickly than usual, to go past, to go alone out onto the empty floor, but Hussein grabbed him and held him. Hussein rapped at the new schedule with his finger, rapped at Andy's name. "Andy is a kid, and all kids are punks. But he doesn't know how to be a waiter which is probably a good thing, so I am happy for Andy that he gets to keep his job. I am even more happy for the other reason. For the reason that O'Meara and Chick lost. Even the general manager, even bigshot Fat Tom that we never see, lost. You kept them from their joke, which means you won, Hero, you motherfucker, and they even gave you the Wednesday night. You did, you beat the rulers. But that was not enough for you. I hear you also made the crazy Bolivian go quiet for a few minutes. How did I miss everything? I am gone for my two days off, and when I come back I have to get you a horse to ride around on because you are a motherfucking hero for real."

Hussein laughed. "I am getting you a horse." Still holding Hero in place, Hussein reached with his free hand and shook Hero's hand. "What do you say to that, Motherfucker?"

Hero had nothing to say.

All his work now, all his attention, had to be focused on his litany. It was as if he had never been invisible, as if he were beginning all over again, and all he could have imagined saying to the Iranian now was the sidework before every service, for each station, front man and back man. Where the fresh bread was delivered, and how hot to set the warmer.

What he did say was, "I had two children."

Hussein slapped him on the shoulder. "Good for you. For that I will get you an extra horse. You beat Chick and O'Meara. You beat the real boss, the hidden Fat-motherfucking-Tom. If I were a young man, I would be fooled all over again. I would take a stand. I would get them to fix the motherfucking toilet downstairs; that's what I would do."

In his enthusiasm he let go of Hero, and Hero tried again to push past and get out alone onto the floor.

"No, Hero. You cannot go away from me. I was a hero once in a while, too, you know. Everybody is a hero once in a while, even the crazy Bolivian. Just because I give you the horses, don't think you are the only George Washington. Because you know what else? You know how many kids I had?"

Hero made no sound.

"I had six sons in my country, Hero. All are dead. In this country now, I have one daughter and she is a first year in college and she tortures me because I am old and stupid and ugly and poor and pay too much attention to her or not enough attention. She tortures me because I am her father. I put up with it because she is smarter than all the others together in that college. Now they want to take away the loans for her college, but she is too smart for all of them and has too much courage. Just like you. You and I, Hero. Yes. That is what we will do. We will start the revolution. Now is the time. We will get them to fix that motherfucking toilet, if we have to kill them all to do it."

The book for Sunday was so slow that Chick had a lottery for the waiters who wanted to go home. Hero did not draw. He wanted to stay, and if it was not going to be busy, he wanted to stay when everyone else was gone. He needed to wrap the shroud of the place around himself as tightly as it had been before. He could do that, and it would be fine again.

When those who were able to go were gone, then Castro came out to the station to tell Hero that he, Castro, could have gone, but had chosen to stay. "I gave my slip to the Yugo," he said. "I thought you needed company because you fought with your beauty. Also, since we got the Frenchman's Wednesday night, I think for a while I will be a man who likes to stay at work. The American way, no? I let Chick see me give away my slip. Next week if I win, I go home to the babies. Or go drink some beers with my new wife."

Then Castro said that he would sit in the kitchen while waiting for customers, if that was all right with Hero.

"Because you want to stand out here alone. *Sí?* You are sad for your beauty. I think you did her wrong, so you deserve sadness. It is no different with me. But after a couple weeks of the Frenchman's Wednesday, we are rich and famous, and my beauty might come back to me, and maybe your beauty will forgive you. Though the ones who pay in cash do not always forgive easily. The Mexican's customer, Three Finger, who is in the mob, he pays in cash also. But I don't think your girl friend is in the mob."

Castro went to sit in the back, and Hero stayed, the only waiter on the floor. He stood with his legs apart and his hands crossed behind his back and he leaned lightly on his hands against the top of the busing stand.

No customers came into the restaurant, and Hero closed his eyes to let the restaurant come into him, to let the litany pour through him and the service surround him when there was nothing to distract. He said aloud the prices of desserts.

Molly said, though it could just as well have been Alice, Molly said, "What about your boys?" It wasn't a question. She knew. Alice knew. Knew everything. As if there was anyone on earth that didn't know. It was an accusation, God damn her.

And Hero smiled. He didn't shout. He told her, and only as he told her did it become a shout.

"I drank everybody to death," he shouted. "And I threw away every penny I ever had. You want to know the details? Except for my youngest boy who got the hell away as quick as he could and as far as he could and never came the hell back. All right? Because I can drink you to death too, and don't you ever think I can't."

There was no answer to that, was there. Just her quiet, so he shouted at her silence, screamed at that. "Don't be sorry for me," he screamed. "You're nobody to be sorry. Look at you, for Christ sake. So mind your own God damn business."

Castro hit Hero on the arm, and Hero opened his eyes and could feel his face tight, his jaws clenched. He was bent at the waist, and he glanced to see if there were customers.

"It's okay," Castro said.

No one was near them, and Hero was as ashamed as if he had been out loud. He might have been out loud, and he looked at Castro to see if Castro had heard.

"You were sleeping," Castro said. "Standing up like a horse. Go sleep in the back on a chair, and I will stand for a while and watch our empty tables."

Hero nodded and went, not to the kitchen but to the desk and the bar. Chick looked up from doodling in the book and said, "You got an appointment, Hero?" and went back to the book without waiting for an answer.

Hero went to the front doors and out to the street.

There, stopped just up from the canopy, was a taxi, and Hero was aware as if for the first time of being actually on the sidewalk he used night after night. Actually in the night, beside brick and asphalt, with thin Sunday night street traffic and the dirty yellow shine of the cab. There were sounds, and the smell of the air was sulfurously clean after the oiled atmosphere of the restaurant. It was cold through his white cotton shortcoat.

He looked for Molly. Up and down the block, the sidewalk on both sides of the street was empty. Was she in the taxi, waiting for him? It would not have felt peculiar for both of them to get in a taxicab and go where they were going.

He pulled the two twenties that she had left and that he had kept, that he had brought back now two nights running — he pulled the twenties out of his pocket and waved them at the cab, which started up and came toward him.

Thank Christ. Molly had come for him and they were finally getting the hell out of here.

As the cab eased up along the curb for him, nothing else mattered. Who cared now? In fact it hadn't mattered for more than twenty years (and even then it had only mattered to him) that he had come from a perfectly respectable family and drunk his way through a good university in the days when respectable families and good universities had to do with ladies and gentlemen. It didn't matter that the last summer he had anything to offer his youngest boy, their yard was on a couple acres. It wasn't more than that; it wasn't fancy in the scheme of those things out the parkway. He hadn't known those people for twenty-five years, and they hadn't wanted to know him for a long time before that. It didn't even matter now that he only knew how to live in two-and-a-half rooms among other people's second-hand furniture.

He had only punched Alice, really punched her, once. It was only right this minute for the first time in a hundred years that he could remember rolling drunk out of bed and shitting in a corner of his own God damned bedroom. In the days when he still had a real bedroom. In the days . . .

It didn't matter because the taxicab picked up speed as it passed him, and whoever was in the back seat was no one Hero had ever seen before. In a moment the cab was around the corner and gone.

And as soon as that, it was done.

All the work Hero had imagined beginning all over again, all the emptying of possibility, all the re-mummifying of emptiness. Done. The street, the night, whatever noises and facades surrounded him, were gone irrevocably back to the familiar and irrelevant walls of his own constant return to service. The street was no more than part of the service, because in this restaurant as in any other, he had every once in a while to walk the terribly important customers, or the distressed ones, outside to a car. That truth folded into his litany and into himself as a blessing.

The only smell on earth now came from himself and his clothing.

Until he stepped back inside the restaurant, where it became the restaurant's smell, the same as Hero and more.

When the restaurant was busy and full of its roar and its satisfactions, then the smell was hidden beneath. But when the restaurant was empty, even purely in the dining room before the beginning of a service when everything had been cleaned, even when Hero had showered and had put on everything clean including a shortcoat fresh from the laundry, still there was the smell of food cooked, and left, of cooking gone cold and greases rancid in the air, in the paint, in the soles of shoes. In the kitchens that smell was tangibly the air itself, and after a service, after bathing in the flood of juices that recharged the air and that congealed onto clothing soaked by the sweat and anxieties of a busy shift, then the smell was putrid, if you were new and if you noticed.

But Hero was not new, and noticed only gratefully. It was the smell of the rest of his life and it was a comfort, the skim which sealed over his numbness now and forever.

As Hero came down along the bar toward the dining room the barman said, "Hero. You're still waving those two twenties around. What's up? No takers on the street either?"

Hero did not answer. He didn't pay attention. The only thing on his mind was the fact that tonight there would not be all the waiters for the sidework at the end of the shift. And if they closed early, most of the waiters still around would clear out at a run. It would be Hero who remembered to gather up the cornucopia of produce spread on the table by the front door, and to take it down to the cold locker.

The barman walked with Hero, along his other side of the bar.

"I like your woman," the barman said. "Every time she comes in she tells Chick to go fuck himself. As soon as he starts to ooze. Next time she comes in, we'll give her something. Find out what she likes."

What who likes? Molly of course. Hero wasn't senile yet. But Molly was gone. A customer who would not be back. Hero went carefully down the three steps to the floor of the dining room, oblivious now to what the barman leaned after him to say.

"She's got a nice step," the barman said. "I've watched her. Thirty years, I hope I'll have a woman walks like that."

ORCHESTRATING THE TOILET

The Iranian began orchestrating the toilet, mentioning it to Chick and then to O'Meara, and, ever so slightly at first, goading the other waiters into outrage.

It was Hussein's theory — and he shared his theory with Hero, insisted that Hero was part of the planning — not to get the waiters worked up too quickly, not to bring the thing to a head before proper momentum had built. There was choreography to a revolution as Hussein understood it.

For background, he gave frequent and guided tours. The green, metal door was swollen away from its hinges and could be drawn only most of the way closed by holding to a coat hanger wound around the inside doorknob. The floor was wet, always. There was a small sink and the water to its taps was shut off so that the sink was black with dirt and overflowing with paper towels. The light did not work, and the mirror over the sink, for its soiled surface and the darkness of the cubicle, cast no reflection. The toilet itself did not flush. The waiters, if they had to piss during the service, stepped in through the puddle to the bowl, and pissed in on the sewage that filled the bowl. The walls were black with filth. The corners, the underneath of the sink, behind the bowl, all were strewn with paper towels, all damp and filthy. None of the waiters admitted using the bowl for more than pissing, but plainly it was more than just the

Chinese dishwashers who did use it. Every ten days or so a plumbing maintenance operation came through as if to repair the toilet, but all that was ever accomplished was to empty the bowl enough to let it be used further. The water on the floor seemed not itself to be sewage, not mostly sewage, but where it came from no one knew.

None of this was new to Hero, and none of it made Hero part of the planning.

None of it was new to the other waiters, although they were part of the theory. Hero was not even part of that.

He stood when the Iranian lectured and cajoled, but Hero had no suggestions. He allowed himself to be dragged to witness the toilet, but he had no outrage. The toilet was a part of his litany, an uncounting marker into and out of service after service. It was a part of the restaurant as Hero was part of the restaurant.

"Are you afraid?" Hussein asked him. "You are. You are frightened of the managers and you want to keep your job. You want to keep your motherfucking Wednesday nights. I thought you were a man, and it turns out your are a coward worse than any of the rest of these. And the rest of these are not much, believe me."

Hero sat on his glass-rack against his wall in the hour before service and nodded, watching between his knees and between his shoes to the red damp of the kitchen floor.

"Good. We don't need cowards. Stay out of it. Maybe they will make you a maître d' like motherfucking Chick."

Then on the floor, Hussein came and stood beside him and whispered, "I know you are not a coward, but you have to wake up because I need you if we are going to do something with these motherfuckers. Not just with Chick and O'Meara and motherfucking Fat Tom wherever he is, but also even with our own motherfucking comrades."

Hero was part of the restaurant, and soon enough the Iranian would not be able to distinguish him from other parts.

And it was no different with the rest. Soon enough he would be invisible again to all of them.

Castro said, "You miss your beauty, Man."

Hero missed nothing. He moved indistinguishably in the passage of every evening's menued service.

"You are sad," the Bolivian said in his hollow voice as he pushed a guéridon through Hero's emptying station. He took one hand from the guéridon and made a ramming motion with his fist and forearm, and said, "Sometimes it is sad," and then laughed and moved on for the kitchen.

The barman said, "What's up, Big Guy? She's not coming back?" and Hero ordered his drinks and set out his fruit.

Andy did not try to sit and eat with Hero, but a number of times he stood near Hero in that hour before the service, and Hero watched at the floor, did not see anyone near him.

It was not busy immediately up to Christmas, and the week between Christmas and New Year's was dead, and then after New Year's began a paced routine, not slow, but without crowds or conventions. This was when Hussein meant to build to his confrontation. Hussein stood by the weekly schedule, between the doors to the dining room, and harangued everyone who passed on the errands of their sidework. He made an event there, announcing revolutionary theory and questioning self-respect and denouncing faults of motherfucking hygiene.

When all of the waiters, all of them but Hero, gathered to laugh in a group just outside the doors, out on the floor, the Iranian shouted through to them from the kitchen, "If you have no self-respect, at least have respect for your assholes. This is America. You are supposed to be clean. Here the revolution works."

Then the waiters tossed knotted napkins in the door from the dining room and made noises of explosion. The Polack shouted, "Hand grenades, Ayatollah. The Iraqis are here."

The Bolivian dodged in, dropped his trousers and bent at the Iranian, calling, "Die, Ayatollah. Die."

"Now this asshole," the Iranian said. "This motherfucking asshole," and one of the other waiters snapped the door open again so that Fedy was knocked over to roll on the floor with his pants around his ankles.

Hero sat on a glass-rack against the wall among ice buckets and beside rubber pails of ice brought up for the service. He listened only to the tenor of their laughter, which told him that there would be no new turbulence.

If there were a difference in Hero's routine, it was that he came in fifteen or twenty minutes earlier than he used to do, so that he might have finished his sidework before Hussein set up between the doors in and out of the dining room. Though the harangue was already shortening, in fact Hero did not mind arriving early.

And he stayed a bit later. Ordinarily, the last waiter on the floor at the end of the night gathered the fruits and vegetables piled decoratively by the front doors, and took them to the cold locker in the downstairs kitchen. Hero would not have minded always taking the last parties, and always being last on the floor, but he couldn't force that on Castro. So now when he and Castro were done, if they did not have the last party, Hero often simply went and stood at the front of the restaurant, near the doors, until the end of the service.

It did not take long for it to be understood that Hero would break down the display of produce, and take it all to the locker, that Hero would be the last man out. He used that time in which he waited for the last party to leave by running his litany. Now there were new dishes on the menu, to know in every aspect. There were new prices to memorize.

Once in a while, if it was late and had been busy, Hero's legs could be tired enough that he leaned, circumspectly, on the last bar stool at the end of the bar. That was not a problem. No customer would be at the bar then, and the barman would be busy at the other end, closing his register. And even leaning on the bar stool, Hero made a grace note for the restaurant at the finish

of the evening, almost unnoticed but there, a humble and man-
nered, final good night.

On one particular night, as the last party left and Hero moved
to collect the fruits and vegetables from their display by the
door, Bogart, who had had that last party, ran down the bar to
stop Hero. An athlete had called and asked to come in, and they
were going to stay open for him. He would be in soon. Bogart
wanted to take him. Bogart offered to take the produce down to
the cold locker so that Hero didn't have to stay, but another hour
or so was nothing to Hero. He leaned on his bar stool.

Bogart went back along the bar toward the floor, to make one
table especially right. Chick and the barman laughed between
the desk and the end of the bar. O'Meara, unseen, shouted
something in his Sambuca voice from his table below and
beyond the desk. Hero watched the doors for a few minutes,
ready to stand when one of the passing cabs stopped. When cab
after cab did not stop, he swiveled on the stool and looked across
the bar into the dark, mirrored forest of bottles.

He had a glimpse of himself in that mirror behind the bottles, and although he already was sitting up straight, he sat
more so. He looked away from himself and the bottles, up into
the dim, distancing seam the mirror made with the ceiling. He
was warm, and he unbuttoned his shortcoat, and immediately
buttoned it again. He put his hands on the bar and searched for
his reflection through the bottles once more, and found it. He
reached again to unbutton his coat and left it unbuttoned, and
then spread and pressed his hands on the bar top.

He looked not much different than he ever had.

It was not as if he didn't have a bathroom in which he shaved
and brushed his teeth and combed what hair he had, there
before that mirror. Hero knew what he looked like, or close
enough. And it was not as if he had never noticed the bottles in
every bar of this and every other restaurant, even when he was
only washing dishes.

He may not have sat on a stool.

And never sat so alone at the end of a shift when the booze was a reek, even in an expensive place like this where people sat at the bar only to wait for tables. Maybe the barman had spilled at this end tonight.

Hero knew who he was and where he was, and yet the halved face looking out from across the dimness and behind the bottles was the face from an other eternity of bars and nights. The same face that learned his oldest son was dead from drugs and said aloud to anybody who wanted to know, in whatever dive he was using, that he didn't give a damn.

The same face, long before that, that he saw reflected in the back window of his own car after he'd come drunk from the train to his youngest boy's little league game. Come in a taxi, halfway through, already in a fury because he'd missed the proper train. A fury at Alice who had had to bring the boy on to the game instead of picking him up. Her fault, he had made that, and her fault, not his, that their son couldn't get a hit when he himself had never even made a team, any team, as a kid. He made Alice drive home without him. He wouldn't ride in the car. He would walk home in his suit. Miles. Without loosening his necktie. As he sent his wife and son and car away without him, he saw the reflection of his fury in the back window, and behind that reflection he saw his son learning not to know him. He saw his boy already past afraid, already learning to look at him and not see him. Years. Years before Alice and her friends, his friends once, began telling the boy he should think of his father as dead. Dead, God damn them, and then they left him.

Hero wanted no drink now and would never want a drink, but the face across the bar looked out from behind the bottles, and looked down the bar.

That familiar face shouted down the bar.

"Bartender."

Shouted it so loud that Hero came absolutely alert to this steakhouse and exactly these bottles and the exact weights of whatever lobsters were available tonight and the multiplied price of each.

"Bartender," he shouted again. Shouted in a fury. "For Christ sake. I need a drink here."

Hero stood up and looked down the bar himself, and the barman was coming, fast, and Hero was afraid. Afraid of what he'd yelled and of everything else.

He stood with his arms at his sides and he watched the face of the barman approaching. But as though nothing had been yelled at all, the barman looked beyond Hero to the front door. He slapped Hero's shoulder so that Hero would look too, and he leaned across the bar next to Hero and said, "I'd like to shake your hand, Sir."

Hero turned to see the third baseman.

The third baseman was dressed in a blue suit, but it could have been no one else, and he shook the barman's hand.

"I've seen an awful lot of them," the barman said, "but you're the only one whose hand I ever really wanted to shake."

"My pleasure," the third baseman said, speaking in just the way he had spoken to the announcer, politely and because he had to. He wanted dinner, and his couple of friends were already going on down the bar, but he had been stopped here next to Hero.

"This is our own Hero," the barman said and laughed. "I mean, that's what we call him, Hero."

The third baseman smiled and, without looking at Hero, said, "He looks like the real thing."

Then he grabbed a paper cocktail napkin from one of the stacks and pulled out a pen. "How about an autograph?" he said. He said that, and wrote the autograph, to get away. To be a nice guy, and still catch up with his pals. In one motion, and even in that little motion you could see the athlete, he wrote, and turned, and started down the bar, and pushed the small paper square of the napkin back along the bar behind him, pushed it to just before Hero on the bar. Without ever having looked at Hero. Without, at least it seemed that way, having looked at what he wrote.

Hero would have given the napkin over to the barman, but the barman was not interested in an autograph. He was keeping up with the third baseman moving down the bar toward the floor. The barman was offering drinks for the whole party, even as Bogart was collecting and shepherding the party, taking over and keeping Chick at a distance.

Above the third baseman's signature, the napkin said, "For Hero and the boys." Hero folded it and put it in his pocket. No reflection came at him from behind the backs of the bottles, and he turned away from the bar and leaned on his stool and waited for this last party to leave so that he could break down the fruits and vegetables.

SUCCESS

A good looking woman, apparently, came through their station, and Castro did not need Hero's notice of her. Andy got a job at another restaurant, at a restaurant, he told Hero, "with other kids and stuff." But once he'd said that, and told the others and given his two weeks' notice, it was done, and whenever any next guy showed up to trail and learn the service he would know Hero only as silence. The toilet was a timeless addition to kitchen myth; napkin hand grenades were an understood part of conversation among the guéridons in that hour before the service when Hero sat invisible on his glass-rack against the wall.

Sometimes when Hero came in as early as he did now, when he turned the corner from the back hall into the stairs, he would see through the hot kitchen to the office, and Chick or O'Meara would be in at that desk. Sometimes he would see the Bolivian leaning against the line in the hot kitchen, because the Bolivian liked to lurk there and hope for a piece of real food before the waiter's regular dinners were put out. Hero never spoke to Chick or O'Meara. He never spoke to Fedy Llosa, or to any of the hot cooks who were at their prep. He went up the stairs and did his own sidework in the empty dining room.

But one night, after leaving his overcoat in his locker and coming in past the baled garbage and past then the damp stink of the toilet and the two corners to the end of the hot kitchen, he heard laughter from the office.

As he began up the stairs he heard a voice which he could identify without recognizing.

"Who's that?"

He was already several quick steps up, well out of sight of the office, before another voice, Chick's, called him back.

He went down the several steps and across the empty front of the hot kitchen to the office door where Chick waited. O'Meara was inside. So was Fat Tom.

Hero had only glimpsed him once or twice, but this was him, and he stood up from behind the desk and smiled at Hero. He said, "Hero. It is you, isn't it. I'm glad to meet you."

Hero stood in the door, just past the cold locker, just before the stacks of trays, with the hot kitchen, with the line, behind him. In a few hours, back men would grab the trays and file along this side of the line to pick up their orders. On the far side of the line, the broiler man and his two other cooks were nearly prepped.

Hero faced into a clutter of filing cabinets and menu blanks and stopped laughter. Fat Tom was more big than fat, with a suit that was too wrinkled and with his necktie loosened. Hero did not look at him more than courtesy demanded, but he saw those things and saw the reddened, pleasant face.

"What I wondered," Fat Tom said. "Was whether you heard what I said. Whether you heard our joke."

Hero stood, and reached one hand lightly to touch at his keys.

"Did you hear what I said? Did you hear the joke?" The voice gained an edge but the smile remained.

Hero shook his head.

"I can't hear you, Hero."

"No," Hero said, and felt his keys, and made himself ready to go away.

"Well. Good. Okay. Thanks for dropping by."

Chick stepped at Hero, and Hero turned from the doorway.

"No," Tom said. "Actually, hold on."

And Chick stepped back, and Hero looked back in the office door. Fat Tom's smile had broadened. He was plenty younger than Hero, but old enough that it didn't make so much difference. He could have played Santa Claus.

He said, "Hero. Yes. Here's an idea. You can do me a favor. Would you? After all, you've recently had a close call. You're still a front man despite some serious odds, and you've even gotten the Wednesday nights. I should think that would make us friends."

Fat Tom paused and studied Hero, and Hero stood, one hand against the bump of keys in his pocket, his eyes aimed at the metal leg of the office desk behind which Tom stood.

"Fine," Tom said. "Here's what I'd like. We've all gotten tired of the talk about the toilet and the thing about napkins and hand grenades. We're going to stop all that. In fact that's what we were laughing about. What I said was, if they want another toilet, they can shit in their mouths. Isn't that funny? And I think it gets the message across. So that's what I'd like you to tell Hussein and the other waiters. Tell them all, for me, that if they want another toilet they can shit in their mouths."

Hero looked down at the same one metal leg of the office desk and waited to understand by the tones of voice and any shift of movements when he should go away.

"Okay? Can you remember that, Hero?"

"Yes," Hero said, ready again to leave.

Fat Tom laughed. "You're not a talker, Hero. A good waiter but not a talker. That's all right. In fact a terrific waiter, if you can carry two stations on a busy night, though why the hell you'd want to do it for the kid is beyond me. What I understand, he had it coming. And now that he's finally learned how to do it, he's quitting for God sake."

Fat Tom paused again.

Hero stood, his hand to the empty safety of his keys, and almost tried to turn away again. There was irritation and impatience in the last of Fat Tom's voice; it did seem that he was through with Hero.

But Chick wanted to say something, and so Hero stood where he was.

"Listen," Chick said. "Hero is not just a good waiter with a soft heart for kids and dogs. He's also got a honey. A honey who tips, isn't that right, Hero?"

"Good," Fat Tom said. "That's what we like to hear." Hero could sense Fat Tom smiling, recognized an agreeable tone of voice. Or was it a voice already too much bored?

Hero worried suddenly that he himself was not paying attention.

Chick said, "Where is she anyway? We haven't seen her for a while. You didn't blow it did you? You don't want to piss on a gravy train like that. No sir. She may not look it, but I bet she could buy us all a ticket if she wanted."

Hero stood and waited. Fat Tom said nothing more.

"Okay, Hero," O'Meara said, and in those words, in that quiet voice was Hero's cue.

Still, he stood where he was, there in the doorway of the office, watching at the grey, chipped, steel leg of the desk.

Fat Tom turned his back to Hero, and Chick said, "Ahoy, Hero. Anchors away."

Hero did not have to hear any more. He knew to go. In his mind the routine of his station was already occupying him: folding and piling the napkins, stacking the ashtrays, stocking the silver, checking for the forks with bent tines that had begun showing up.

With his back to Hero, with a voice nearly as pleasant as before, Fat Tom said, "Get him the fuck out of here."

But Hero did not go, did not move, and Chick put a hand on his arm to turn and push him out. Which made sense. It made sense even for it to be a careless, abrupt push. Hero didn't care about that.

He did turn.

And he did go.

It had not taken long.

He was still early enough. Nobody really expected him to say anything to the waiters.

He would hurry with his sidework and with setting up the station.

HERO AT LAST

But he'd waited too long.

He'd waited too long to turn and go. He didn't know why he had, but he had, and now Fat Tom was shouting.

"You," Fat Tom shouted, and he was shouting at Hero.

Because Hero had turned away, because he was obliged to look back into the office, he could see Fat Tom now leaning across the desk at him.

Could see Fat Tom's face.

And Fat Tom was angry for the first time. Shouting for the first time.

Which was all it took. That rage and its noise.

Hero knew him.

Fat Tom shouted, "Are you deaf? I said, Get the fuck out of here."

Hero didn't need to hear that, didn't need to hear any more at all.

He had recognized Fat Tom.

Fat Tom was not drunk this minute, but Fat Tom was a drunk.

A God damned drunk.

Hero had known assholes like Fat Tom in every gin mill on earth.

Known them and hated them.

With a propulsive exuberance as furious as pleasure Hero pushed back past Chick.

"I know you," he shouted into Tom's livid face. He held his keys in his hand, in a fist, not knowing how they'd gotten there, and he shouted. He shouted, and it was a real noise he made this time, "I know you."

For a moment Fat Tom was surprised. He gazed at Hero as if actually trying to place where they might have met.

Chick and O'Meara, wondering themselves, gazed back and forth between Hero and Fat Tom.

Then Fat Tom smiled. A smile of hatred and dismissal.

It was not enough. Hero knew him for a drunk. And Fat Tom knew that Hero knew. Chick and O'Meara must have known as well, because Fat Tom turned to them and they made no move to throw Hero out. Fat Tom would have to do it himself, and Hero was not afraid of that. He stood his ground.

Fat Tom said quietly, ominously, as if a tone of voice could possibly be enough, "Get away from me you worn out old sack of shit, before I tell them to use you for the toilet."

Not quietly — not shouting, but louder than Fat Tom, loud enough that everyone in that room would know — Hero said, "I want to tell you that I'm calling the health department in the morning about the toilet and the lockers. I'm also calling the union. And when they get here, I'm going to ask if we can shit in your mouth until the repairs are done."

Then he threw his keys. Not drunk, but as good as drunk. Threw his keys at that other drunk, that red-faced fraud, threw them as hard as he could, like a God damned baseball player, to kill him. And the keys hit one of the filing cabinets and Hero didn't care. He'd said it, and already turned and left for good.

Halfway up the stairs he heard Fat Tom laugh.

In another minute or so Chick and O'Meara came through the dining room and said nothing to Hero.

But before the service, when the other waiters had finished their sidework and their dinners and sat among the guéridons, when Hero sat across from them on his glass-rack, Chick came into the kitchen to say that from now on Castro would work the front and Hero would be a back man.

Hero did not answer the other waiters' questions. He went downstairs to the hot kitchen and got a tray and walked back up the stairs. He held the tray out from his stomach, and walked up that way without sight of the individual steps. He went up and down three times in succession, and then went to the head of the line where the trays were loaded, and with the empty tray out from his stomach, counted the paces to the stairs, and then went up those, and came back down and began again at the head of the line. The broiler man and the grill man and the third man, all stared at him. "What you been taking, Hero?" the broiler man, the lead man, called at him. "You going to share with your friends downstairs?"

Hero nodded, and went back upstairs and sat on his glass-rack for the time left. He ran all of his downstairs litany again in complete absorption. To remember it? There was no need to remember. Monkey of béarnaise, monkey of hollandaise, melted butter, curled lemon, watercress, parsley. Plotting on the trays for space and balance; the main course round, the monkeys, the covers, the double servers and single servers, the stack fits, the napkins between stacking. It was all there. Hero ran it to cement the assumption that it all would get done. Hero did not hear the doubt. He did not hear the voices of the other waiters. He swam in his litany, and it was familiar, cozy, even if it was a back man's litany. He was home. He felt none of the attention of the other waiters, their rustle around him. The Bolivian came and stood beside him and put a hand on Hero's bare, bald head, and said, "My heroine," with his eerie voice which pronounced heroine perfectly. Then Fedy went off, and in a few minutes came back and put his hand again on Hero's head and must have looked to the waiters for their approval, because there was a general giggle. "My heroine," he said again. Hero looked through his own black shoes at the red concrete floor. Like a river, he ran a whole night's litany. When the Bolivian moved off, Hero pressed with the heels of his hands along the tops of his thighs.

It was a Saturday night, but it would not be a busy one. "I will space them out," Castro told him. "I don't know what happened, but we make it no problem," Castro said. Hero nodded and checked their tables, checked the guéridon Castro had fitted up before they changed positions, put his own name on the guéridon's top cloth.

It did begin slowly. Couple of deuces. A single. A three. Hero handled them. There was not space between litany and the physical ritual. Whenever he had a moment, Hero went to the kitchen and sat against his wall and rubbed the heels of his hands against his thighs. At those moments, even as he rubbed, he tried to relax his arms. He also listened to his chest. He relaxed his jaws from the grinding of teeth at the back of his mouth.

He waited, but he didn't have to wait long, didn't have to wait for what Chick and O'Meara could arrange.

There was a four, another four, the three turned for a four, the single to a deuce, and the station was full; the floor was full, and everyone was running. It was an instant hit, so that all the floor closed up at once and the kitchen backed up and the dishwashers backed up. Silver had to be grabbed out of the rinse. Aids was behind and had to be pampered and urged. The tables had to be turned and cleared and reset. Hero could manage all this. But when the restaurant was hit all at once, you could not come down to the line and pick up only one table at a time. All the orders came through at once, all the customers sat and waited at once. All the other waiters came and stood waiting on their side of the line for food to come up. You went down and picked up everything that the cooks could give you. If they gave you three fours, you took three fours, or else you went home.

Only once did Hero feel for his keys, quickly and in the rush of everything, but they were not there and he did not feel for them again.

He went down and got two trays, to double up. He was not afraid. He stood in line behind the other waiters, holding his trays, holding his napkins to keep the plates from sliding. He checked his dupes. He figured what would come over the counter in what order so he could arrange and balance. He counted hollandaise and béarnaise. When he was two back from the head of the line, the third cook, sweating, jabbering, ladling, called, "Here come's the Hero now. Muscles abursting."

When he was next to the head of the line Hero called his tables to the lead man, the broiler man, who pulled down their dupes and called the plates. Then it was Hero at the head of the line, and he laid his trays out and the plates began coming, slung to him by the lead man. Hero grabbed them and threw in the parsley and watercress and covered them. He stacked the monkeys in the center, threw napkins over to double up top, and crossed two main course covers with a double server of onion rings. Hero was not afraid. Even as he handled the individual plates, he felt their weight. Of course he would not be able to carry.

Other hands reached for his plates. The waiter behind, and Hero could not be distracted enough even to know who it was, loaded Hero's other tray so that Hero would go faster, so that the waiter behind would get his own order sooner. Hero tried only to watch out the side of one eye to be sure that tray was stacked so it would not slide. He would never carry it all. He raced to cover his vegetable sides, and tucked them in at the corners of the tray. The hands next to him grabbed fast and with the same hurry of the night. The push of urgency came from all down the line. Hero concentrated on the stacking, making it tight, knowing that the moment it was done, he would pick up and turn away and go. He would turn and all would go to the floor. He might get a step, two steps. He would rather have loaded the second tray himself, to be sure it was right; it was already doubled up on top. He turned to finish that tray. His response to the urgency was his own careful urgency to throw it all on the floor. He studied the balance on the second tray, gauged the fit to the top of the stacking of his first tray.

"Go, Man," the waiter behind him ordered. "Take your motherfucking tray."

Hero moved at the second tray to lift it to the top of his first tray. The lead cook was shouting out the plates for the waiter behind, and Hero set himself to lift and stack his second tray, but the waiter behind shoved him away from it. The hollow voice shouted from close range through Hero's blind splicing of litany, ritual and impossibility, "Go, Man. What the fuck's wrong with you? Take one fucking tray."

The third cook yelled with the frenzy of too much business, "The Hero taking ludes, not trays."

It was Fedy Llosa behind Hero, and now his wildly jawed face was furiously into Hero's face.

"Move your ass, Hero," the broiler man shouted as he began slinging the next plates.

Hero picked up his first tray, and left the second.

He walked the exact paces to the stair bottom. Even the one tray, doubled up as it was, was too heavy for him. He counted the paces. At the stairs he stepped up, feeling for the top of the first step, oblivious to the enormous, tunneled height of all the steps above him.

His foot would not come high enough to find the top of the first step. The toe of his shoe slid against the face of the first step. His legs quivered, and began to empty of muscle. He did not look up into the height and steepness. He willed the one foot to come up and it would not. His arms stiffened, and the weight of the plates pressed back against his stomach. He could feel the heat through his jacket. One plate came against the thumb of his right hand, and was hot enough to burn cold.

"Move Motherfucker, move." The Bolivian's voice came like a foghorn. The edge of a tray, Fedy Llosa's tray, came against

Hero's back, pushing him ahead; either to go up, or to fall into the collapse of his scalding food. He slid his toe up the face of the first step, and could not find the top. The step was too high. The Bolivian's tray pressed hard into his back now, pushing him down, into the stairs. "Go Motherfucker." Hero pushed his toe ahead as though he could force his own hold into the concrete. His other leg could not hold him erect.

He fell.

And falling, his foot reached the top of the first step.

His weight plunged onto that foot, and still falling, he stepped again, and stepped again, up, falling up the stairs.

He hugged his tray against his stomach. He surrounded his plates and servers with his arms and his chest. Sauces, vegetable water, liquid from the fish, all washed over the tray and soaked his cuffs up to his elbow, soaked the front of his jacket through to his stomach. He went up step, up step.

"Up Motherfucker. Up Motherfucker," came Fedy Llosa's commands. "Up Motherfucker," and Hero did go up.

Before he could realize the truth of it, he was all the way up and leaned the two paces around the doorway to his waiting guéridon and set the tray down. Behind came Fedy with the second tray, with Hero's other tray. "Go Motherfucker," Fedy said. "Drive your fucking car," and then Fedy had turned and gone back down the stairs calling as he dove from sight, "Drive the fucking car, Heroine."

It was a busy night, and it did not stop, but even when he doubled tables, Hero had no other pickup as large as that worst one, and no one tray as heavy. And at every pickup after that, the waiter next behind him, the Yugoslav, Henke, even Robert who was so skinny he should not have been able to carry anything, always the waiter behind Hero took off two or three or four plates to carry, and if he had no room, handed a couple to a waiter farther behind. There was no talking, no thanking; it was too busy. But they helped him, and Hero came up with lightened loads. He counted his paces and counted his steps up and set his trays down on the smeared and sopping linen of his guéridon, and then the waiters behind handed off his other plates and he rolled out to the station and served with Castro, and cleared and reset and plated and served appetizers and desserts, and backed Castro whenever there was a moment for that, and had no moment whatever for sitting.

Then there were clear spaces of effort and gaps in the loudness. Turn and no more turn. They would be done. Half the station was reset and empty. Hero kept his pace to get the weight of the last tables through, but he was out the other end of the night. He went to the bar. O'Meara was at his front table with the wads of checks and the bowl of Sambuca. Chick was at the coat check, taking last bucks from a roller.

"You okay?" the barman asked Hero. "They put you in back. You look like war."

Hero looked little different than his fouled guéridon. He said, "Everybody helped me. Can I take a couple of six-packs?"

"Really? The fairies too? Fedy? Too much, Hero. All of a sudden you've got friends. We get your woman back in here and you'll be a prominent fucking citizen." The barman looked down to Chick at the coats, to O'Meara. "Chick is oozing and O'Meara's gone. Sure, why not."

He bent beneath the bar, came up with the six-packs and handed them across to Hero, who held them stacked up his wet stomach and took the three steps to the floor sideways, away from O'Meara, and then went in a line for the kitchen.

Even as Hero came through the tables, the floor emptied of waiters. In the kitchen he tossed one bottle to Aids, two to the dishwashers, and set the rest down for the waiters to open and pour into soup cups. "Up Motherfucker, up Motherfucker," the Bolivian shouted, laughing with panted hysteria as he slopped down the beer. As all of them drank, Hero threw their bottles in under the far garbage, and was out on the floor with the first of them before anyone could have realized.

O'Meara, however, from his table below the desk, pointed across the dining room at Hero, and waved Hero over.

Hero's keys were on the table, and O'Meara said, "Put 'em in your pocket and keep your mouth shut. Also, next time you buy everybody beer, do me a favor and fucking pay for it."

By the next night, and it was a Sunday night, workmen had been into the pit and the toilet. The lockers were moved to the boiler room until a proper room was fixed up. A door had been opened to an adjoining basement so the waiters could use another toilet while the old one was being fixed.

O'Meara, it seemed, had telephoned the owner and told him about waiters maybe calling the union and the health department.

And that news, because Fat Tom was already apparently on thin ice, because Fat Tom was in fact a drunk, that news from O'Meara had been enough to get Fat Tom fired, enough to get the work begun.

That timely news might even have put O'Meara in line for the job of general manager, although O'Meara contended such a possibility had never occurred to him in going to the owner behind Fat Tom's back.

All of which Hussein had already learned from the barman and Chick, and from O'Meara himself.

Learned by the time Hero came in. Because Hero did not come in early. Hero came in at the same time the latest of the waiters came. He came in expecting to be fired.

He came upstairs from the lockers this next night, this Sunday night, and Fedy Llosa jumped up on a chair and shouted, "I am so excited I have to take my clothes off. All you gays turn your heads. You too Heroine." Fedy unbuttoned his shirt, and beneath it he wore a tee shirt which said, "Eat shit and die." Fedy pounded his feet on the seat of the chair, and everyone howled, and through the noise Fedy shouted, "You see that, Heroine?"

Fedy had been in the hot kitchen early the night before, and although he had not heard everything, he had heard what Hero had said finally.

"Shit in the mouth," the Chinese dishwashers called over their long, stainless sink. "Shit in the mouth."

So it was not until the end of the service that Hero could give the autograph to Andy.

He had brought the autograph in because it was Andy's last night and because for all he could have known it was to be his own last night as well.

But the kitchen was loud before the service, and the service itself was busy for a Sunday night.

Only when things had slowed at the end of the service could Hero, at the back of the dining room, near the kitchen doors, give Andy the napkin that the third baseman had signed. Andy knew who it was, knew the third baseman had been in. Andy was glad to have it, and Hero said, "Good luck."

And the Bolivian saw.

Fedy Llosa waved the other waiters over from their emptying stations. He called to them in a shouting whisper as they gathered, "Look. The Hero is giving a note to Andy. The Hero can't bear to lose Andy's cock forever."

Fedy grabbed the napkin from Andy, and as the other waiters closed and circled, he cried, "It is a love letter."

"Don't take it," Castro said, and Fedy handed the napkin to the Polack.

Fedy said, "It is a love letter from the Hero to Andy. It says everything Hero did he did for Andy."

Robert took the napkin and said, "It's an autograph, you dumb fuck. It says, For Hero and the boys. From Bogart's dipshit baseball player we had to hear so much about."

"That's what I said," Fedy shouted. "Who are the other boys, Hero? Besides Andy? I am so jealous I can't stand it."

Hussein grabbed the napkin from Henke, and said, "They are Hero's sons. What's the matter with you, Bolivian? Can't you give the man one night's respect?"

"I am too jealous," Fedy said.

"I was married," Hero said.

And the laughter among the other waiters subsided.

"I had my own house," Hero said. "I had two sons."

"A long time ago, I bet," the Polack said. "You drink it all away?"

"What difference does that make?" Hussein said. "Don't ask him that, Motherfucker."

"You still have your sons," Castro said. "A father always has his sons."

"That's right," Hussein said. "Don't pay any attention to this Bolivian motherfucker."

"Do you know where they are?" Robert said.

"How dare you," Bruce said. "How dare you think such a thing about Hero's boys."

Hero said, "I live here now."

And again the laughter went quiet.

Fedy put his arm around Hero's shoulders.

Castro said, "You still have your sons, Hero. No matter what."

"It is true," Fedy said. "You still have your sons, Hero."

He said it seriously, and the other waiters looked at Hero with silent, uncomfortable curiosity.

"And you know what else you have?" Fedy said. He squeezed his arm around Hero's shoulders, and looked among the faces of the other waiters, who remained silent.

"You also have us," Fedy said.

"Us?" Hussein said.

Hussein shouted, "Now he has *us*?"

And Fedy Llosa leaped away from Hero to dance in one kitchen door and out the other.

"Now he has us," Fedy cried into the newest laughter.

After that, Hero did one more peculiar thing.

When Andy was long gone and O'Meara had not gotten general manager, when routine had settled into itself and "Shit in his mouth" had become daily vocabulary unconnected to memory, then one night instead of sitting on a glass-rack by himself against his wall, Hero sat down in the hour before service with the other waiters, among the guéridons.

"Look," Fedy Llosa said. "The heroine is trying to integrate. He is coming to sit in the front of the bus. We have to call the police and the dogs."

The Iranian looked down the kitchen from the schedules, and said, "The front of the bus? You are crazier than I ever realized, Bolivian. You think you are in the front of the motherfucking bus?"

Hero sat in a chair among the other waiters and their guéridons.

And the Polack called, "You think it is camel drivers in front?"

A NOTE ON THE AUTHOR

Frederick G. Dillen was born in New York City
in 1946, grew up in Connecticut, graduated from
Stanford University, and has worked as a waiter
from San Francisco and Sacramento to Gloucester,
Massachusetts and New York City. He now lives and
writes in Santa Fe, New Mexico. *Hero* is his first
published novel.

A NOTE ON THE BOOK

The text for this book was composed by Steerforth
Press using a digital version of Walbaum, a typeface
designed by Justus Erich Walbaum in the early
nineteenth century. The book was printed on acid
free papers and bound by Quebecor Printing~Book
Press Inc. of North Brattleboro, Vermont.